LIGHTING THE FLAMES

A HANUKKAH STORY

SARAH WENDELL

Print cover designed by Kanaxa
Front cover designed by Mollie Smith and Sarah Wendell
Photograph by Nosnibor137
Edited by Angela James
Copyedited by Sara Brady

To Adam

And to everyone who loves and misses summer camp.

CHAPTER ONE

Tuesday, December 16, 2014—24 Kislev 5775

Jeremy Gold stood up from his sunscreen-stained canvas lawn chair, now anchored deep into a pile of plowed snow, and pulled Genevieve up to stand with him.

"A moment of silence for the shit-sucker, if you please."

"It's not the same when it's this cold out," Gen grumbled, rubbing her gloves together and stomping her feet. A small tanker truck rolled past them toward the slowly opening gate that marked the main entrance to Camp Meira. The driver waved at them both, then revved the engine to push through the snow on either side of the road. The plow hadn't left a path quite wide enough for his truck.

Gen looked up from the pattern she'd been stamping with the treads of her boots, remembering something she wanted to tell Jeremy, but when she saw the side of the truck she started to laugh. The company had upgraded since the previous summer. A sign that had clearly once belonged to a Jiffy Lube now read, thanks to creative use of black marker and white duct tape, "Jiffy Latrine."

"That must have taken some work," Gen said, nudging Jeremy.

Jeremy had bowed his head in his typical gesture of respect to the Jiffy Latrine cleaning visit, which amounted to a twenty-minute drive to all three portable toilets in camp. When he raised his head and saw the sign, he began laughing so hard he could barely stand up.

"Now, Jer, that's hardly respectful."

"It's *Jiffy Lube*!"

He bent forward, resting his hands on his knees to try to catch his breath between howls of laughter. His position brought his face down from his normal stratosphere, and Gen watched as tears curled his eyelashes before she looked away.

Then he silenced abruptly, his face serious. "I must have that sign."

"No."

"I MUST. It is imperative."

"No."

"You must aid me in pursuit of the shit-sucker's Jiffy sign!"

"I will do no such thing. Sit your behind down in your chair and wait for the bus."

"You dare question my authority? I outrank you."

"You outrank me? In what dream?" Gen turned to face him, her hands on her hips. She was biting the inside corners of her lips to keep from smiling.

"I've been staff for longer than you."

"Yeah, you and your long staff. So impressive." Gen sat back down in her canvas chair, rolling her eyes. "And yet, you're out here with me on freezing bus detail. Shouldn't you have a more important job, oh highly ranked one?"

"Yes. And I do. Acquisition of the Jiffy Latrine sign."

"You're nuts. Have fun with that. I'm going to sit here and pretend it's August." Or July, when the air was thick and humid and relentlessly hot. When she never had a good hair day, no matter what her hair products promised. When she spent three straight months wearing a ball cap with a ponytail pulled through the back loop, leaving her with a nearly permanent crease across the back of her head. When it was never quiet or still, when there were campers everywhere and noise and laughter and the smells of marshmallows, campfires, and—depending on the direction of the wind—horse poop followed her all day. When all those things combined into the sensory distraction that felt like home. Since her parents had died, camp was the most familiar home she had within reach.

Jeremy wasn't being the distraction she'd expected, though. She'd hoped that during the few days of Winter Camp, their friendship could go back to being normal and easy, and she could pretend like he'd never kissed her, like they hadn't been apart for more than a year with things unfinished and unsaid. They'd covered up the unanswered questions with a mountain of status updates, texts, e-mail, messages, and digital snapshots, which were meaningful since they kept her connected to Jeremy across oceans and time zones, but meaningless in that they didn't talk about what had really happened, and what might have changed.

Jeremy seemed to be acting like his usual giant, goofy self. Maybe he'd forgotten that they'd kissed in the first place.

"You dream of August. I'll dream of my new sign." Jeremy folded his arms over his chest and grinned down at her. With her sitting and him standing at full height with his horribly perfect posture, it was like trying to look up at the sun—painful yet difficult to look away.

"You're nuts, Jer," Gen said, shaking her head and curling into a ball in her lawn chair, desperate for any kind of warmth. Maybe yoga would help. The kind of yoga where she lit her chair on fire, hid under four blankets, and drank from a flask.

"The Jiffy Latrine shall be mine! It will be *epic*!" Jeremy raised his arms and bellowed into the forest, startling two birds from their branches and causing snow to fall directly onto Gen's head.

"What the—Jeremy!" With a growl, Gen launched herself from her chair, tackled Jeremy around the midsection, and drove him backward into a snow pile. His surprise gave her an advantage, but it was only momentary.

"You dare attack the latrine pirate? You shall pay!" Since he outweighed her by at least an additional person's worth of pounds, it was no big deal for Jeremy to toss Gen into the snow pile beside him.

But he didn't anticipate Gen coming up armed with chunks of very tossable snow and hurling them at his head with a yell. "Never! I defend the rightful signage of the Jiffy Latrine!"

"Rightful, my ass!" Dodging both of Gen's snowballs, Jeremy built a mammoth snow missile of his own and fired at her. She ducked, rolled past him, and tried to gain her feet long enough to run past him to the chairs. He grabbed her around the waist, hauled her into the air and spun her around.

"*You're* an ass!" She tried to escape, but he was too strong, and she was laughing too hard.

"And my rightful ass is incomplete! The Jiffy Latrine shall be mine, and you shall help me attain my booty!"

Jeremy moved to toss her into another snowbank left behind by the plow, but he lost his balance and fell. Gen landed under him, both of them buried past their shoulders in a slanted drift of snow.

"Oh, crap, Gen, did I hurt you?" Jeremy looked horrified, lifting his body away from hers. She rolled to her side, bracketed in the space between his arms, sheltered beneath his chest and suddenly in no need of a flask or any blankets. His proximity was enough to set her on fire.

Then his hands slipped and he landed on her again.

His face was so close to hers, she could only see parts of it at a time. His eyelashes, curled with tears from laughing. His beard, which he'd grown in the time she'd been away, a mix of red, brown, and gold, now with a frosting of snow.

He laughed, but it sounded strained. Jeremy's cheeks above his beard were already red from the cold, but they burned even deeper when he managed to steady himself and caught her staring at him.

He opened his mouth, and she heard him draw a breath to reply, but he was cut off by the sound of another engine coming down the camp road. He stood up and quickly pulled Gen to her feet. Looking at the ground, at themselves, at the road, and not at each other, they pushed wads of wet, clinging snow from their arms and legs.

"Great. We're going to welcome ten families into camp like we're the abominable snow couple." Gen closed her eyes, feeling her own face burn. Great. She'd just made things more awkward. But Jeremy didn't seem to notice or care that she'd called them a couple.

"Excellent. Now you'll have to help me score the Jiffy sign."

"Why, spousal duties?" She gave up worrying about what she'd said. It was easier to laugh and joke they way they always had instead of thinking twice or three times about what she was going to say.

"Yeah. Doodies."

"You are so twelve."

"Great! Then I get presents 'cause it's bar mitzvah time."

"Yeah, today you are a man. A snow man. Get your own sign, Frosty."

Then she felt a touch behind her head. Jeremy had removed his glove and was pulling snow from her hair with gentle fingers. It felt like her hair had nerve endings, the feeling of him carefully removing ice from between the dark curls sending tingles over her head and down her back.

Sure, she'd be able to pretend like nothing had happened between them, while his touch made her jump like she'd scuffed her socks on the carpet and touched a light switch. No big deal.

She stepped back, out of his reach, and grabbed her hair with both hands, shaking the rest of the snow away. They almost looked like responsible staff members when a red SUV stopped in front of them.

Scott, the camp director, lowered the window, and Gen saw his smile freeze with a coating of horror when he felt the cold air hit his skin.

"Ready for Winter Camp?" Scott's voice was as awkward as the grin on his face.

"Think so." Jeremy casually formed a snowball in his gloves as he looked toward the camp gate, a large metal barrier that kept people out more than it kept the horses and children inside. It had closed automatically behind the Jiffy Latrine truck and wouldn't open again until it was triggered.

"Don't even think about it, Jeremy," Scott said, glancing at Jeremy's hands.

"Me? Throw a snowball into your nicely appointed and very attractive car? After you made a special trip out to get snacks for our cabin? Never. I'd *never* do such a thing."

Jeremy tossed his snowball from one hand to the other, grinning at Scott.

"Did you get the heat to come on?"

Jeremy's grin didn't falter, but he stopped playing catch. "Yup. All cabins closest to the dining hall have heat, and the thermostats are set to keep them warm. I have it on my schedule to check them every few hours."

Scott nodded, glancing out the windshield as he pressed a button on the remote attached to his visor to open the gates. The metal arms of the gate made slow progress through the snowdrifts, but they were slow moving in the summer, too, when the road was clear beneath them.

"Gen, I got your supplies for s'mores."

"Thanks."

"You are such a chocolate snob."

"Sure am."

Jeremy looked between them, confused. "S'mores?"

"I'm staying in your cabin," Gen replied.

"Our cabin?" Jeremy's eyes widened, like he was horrified. That did wonders for her confidence, but she didn't let it show in her voice.

"Water pipes burst in the girls' bunkhouse. Everything is soaked."

"One more thing to fix," Scott said to no one in particular.

Jeremy still looked aghast at the idea.

"Why, is something wrong? Did you have someone coming to stay with you?"

"Stay? What? No. No one." Jeremy tugged off his cap and rubbed the top of his head with one hand. Then he smiled, bright and eager. "This'll be great. Assistance in pursuit of merriment and Jiffy!"

"Jiffy? You need peanut butter, too?"

"No, not peanut butter. Don't worry about it, Scott." Gen moved in front of Jeremy and when Scott looked away, she elbowed him in the side.

He opened his mouth to protest, but the low rumble and creak of the gates stopped, and the silence interrupted him. They all turned to look. The gates stood only half-open, but high ridges of snow had collected beneath each arm.

"Well, that's not good," Jeremy said, his voice dry.

"Come on, Mr. Snow Man." Gen pushed past Jeremy, but took his arm to pull him along with her. They started clearing the snowdrifts from beneath the metal bars with their hands, kicking the heavy gates open bit by bit. When the gates were finally pressed into the snowbanks on the side of the road, they were both breathing heavily, but the gate motor didn't restart.

Scott drove through but then parked his car in the road and got out. He stood, looking toward the top of the hill, where the dirt road hit the blacktop that eventually curled through the nearest town, then at the silent gate.

"Can you fix it?"

Jeremy shrugged. "Probably. But we're supposed to get more snow tonight or tomorrow, so they'd likely get stuck again. They're not meant to open against snow and ice."

"They're meant to withstand impact from a vehicle. Snow shouldn't be a problem," Scott answered, rubbing his hand on his face.

Jeremy wandered closer to the gatepost, examining the enclosure that housed the motor and the remote sensor. "I can take a look at it, but it'll have to be later, since—"

Scott's worry interrupted him. "If the families drive into camp and the gates are open and no one's here, that's a terrible first impression."

"We're already here to welcome them," Gen replied, incredulous. Did Scott think they were hanging out by the road for fun, that they didn't each have a to-do list with fourteen million things on it? "We'll send the buses straight in, then close the gates manually. They won't notice."

Jeremy looked over his shoulder at her, his eyebrows raised in surprise. He was trying to pry the black metal cover off the motor, with little success.

"And we don't need to leave once we're here," Genevieve continued. "If there's an emergency, we can take the fire road, but we shouldn't have to leave camp more than once this week. The gates usually stay closed anyway."

Scott looked at Gen, then at the gates. He nodded slowly, and climbed back into his car. "The buses should be here in a half an hour or so."

"Aye, sir!" Jeremy saluted as Scott started his car and drove away from them.

After Scott's car disappeared around the bend and the silence surrounded them once more, Gen followed Jeremy back to their chairs, which, thanks to their battle, were covered with fist-sized tufts of snow. Gen tried to brush it off but ended up smearing white all over the canvas.

"He's uptight about something," Jeremy said quietly.

"He's always uptight about something. Comes with the job, I think."

Jeremy sat down, undisturbed by the cold clumps of ice on his chair.

He folded his arms across his chest, one hand pulling at his beard. Gen watched his hand, her eyes following the line of his profile as he frowned, deep in thought. When he glanced over and caught her staring, he turned and faced her. His expression was serious, thoughtful in a way she hadn't really seen him before.

"The gate not working shouldn't be that big of a deal. He was really wigged about it."

"The gate's important. It keeps us safe, and sends a message that we're paying attention to security."

Jeremy shrugged. "There's a cop outside our synagogue on Rosh Hashanah, too. He doesn't do much. Not sure what message that sends, other than, *Hey, we're watching. With one dude.*"

"That's the point." Gen repositioned her chair alongside his but didn't sit down.

"Few people know we're here in the summer," Jer continued. "No one expects us to be here in the winter. What's the big deal?"

"No idea. But either way, we'll operate the gate manually. It'll be our workout for the day."

"Yes!" Jeremy's roar made her look at him, and his silly grin made her smile instantly, like a reflex. After months apart, every summer they fell into the rhythm of the previous year. Maybe this week wouldn't be so difficult. If she could stop herself from staring at him so much.

"My manly strength shall protect us all!"

"Just keep the heat on, big guy," she said, shoving him in the shoulder.

"Wench! I have not forgotten!" He grabbed her arm and pulled her onto his lap. Even with layers of clothing, parkas, ski pants, and more between them, she could feel the firmness of his body, and without thinking about it, she grabbed onto his shoulders, holding tight.

His grin took over his entire face, and the muted sunlight behind the clouds didn't stop the gold and brown in his beard from catching her attention. Then his smile began to slip, just a little. She forced her eyes up to his.

He was staring at her mouth.

She wet her lips with the tip of her tongue before she spoke. "You haven't forgotten what?"

He shifted suddenly, almost like a flinch, and leaned away from her, his happy expression back in place. "You. Me. Sign. We must complete our mission!"

"That's your mission, dude." She pushed herself off his lap and moved to her own chair, telling herself that the cold wasn't that bad, that it hadn't really been that much warmer in the moment when she'd been on his lap, or beneath him in the snow.

"It is our mission." He nodded with the kind of confidence told Gen he wasn't about to forget.

Jeremy never forgot anything.

A little while later, Gen tossed her duffel inside the door of the room she'd chosen and started to unpack. Her wardrobe for eight weeks in the summer was easy: shorts, T-shirts, a few sweatshirts, a hat, sunscreen, and bug spray. Winter meant three times as many clothes for less than a week, including base layers, leggings, pants, long-sleeved shirts, sweaters, and socks so thick she could only wear them with boots.

She pulled off one of her shirts and tossed it over a chair, one of the only pieces of furniture in the room. She and Jeremy had several physical layers between them now, in addition to the awkwardness that she felt lurking beneath their otherwise normal conversations. Maybe she was the only one who sensed the way they didn't fit so easily together anymore. Maybe the awkwardness only existed for her because she still thought about the last time they'd been together at Meira. Last year, when he'd worked half a summer then left before the second session began.

The night he'd left, he'd found her in the art shack, where she worked and pretty much lived between June and August. She'd been sitting on a table, untangling a knotted lanyard that a first-year camper had made and woven incorrectly. She could fix it and show him the right way, but undoing what he'd done in frustration was taking forever.

She'd looked up when Jeremy entered, the screen door swinging behind him. He caught the door before it slammed shut, a sound he knew she hated. She'd turned her attention back to her hands and hadn't noticed anything different until he stood in front of her, so close that his clothing brushed her skin. She could feel his tension and his unhappiness hitting her like waves knocking against the sides of a canoe.

"I'm going home," he'd said, his voice quiet and level and sad.

Gen had sat up, staring at him in shock. "What? Did you get fired? Did they find out about the golf cart? That it was us? Oh, no, no. I'm going to talk to Scott."

She'd dropped the lanyard on the table and reached out to push him back so she could jump off the table to the ground. Jeremy had grabbed her hand, and she'd stopped moving.

"I'm not fired. I got into this program. I was going to start in January, but…" He stopped, then started again. "Someone quit and a spot opened up."

She remembered confusion and sadness and hurt, so much hurt, because nothing he said made sense. He hadn't told her anything about a program, about school, about any of it.

"Where are you going?"

"New York." He'd been so vague, so unwilling to share anything, that the hurt had smothered every other feeling until all she could do was stare at him as he held her hand and watched her face.

"I leave for Iceland in August. Will you—"

"I won't be back by then. I don't come home until December."

"Can I come see you before I go?"

He'd stilled, his eyes unfocused for a moment. Then he'd shaken his head slowly. "No. But I'll see you when you get back."

"Jeremy. I'll be gone for a year. I won't be back until next summer."

"Then I'll see you…then." He'd tried to smile, but gave up. The grin that usually encompassed his face faded before it reached his eyes.

"I don't get it. Why didn't you tell me? What school are you going to?"

He'd stepped closer and dropped her hand, then ran his fingers down the side of her face, over her cheek, then down her neck. She'd been so surprised she hadn't moved, the hurt dulled by the shock of feeling Jeremy touch her like that.

"I will tell you everything, all about it, once I get there. I didn't plan this—it was a last-minute thing."

She hadn't been able to think of a word to say. She'd just stared at him. His hand had come to rest on her shoulder, and his thumb was tracing the edge of her neck where her pulse was beating in triple time.

"I promise I'll explain it, but I—I'm sorry."

He had leaned in, probably to kiss her cheek, but she'd turned her head and kissed him on the mouth. She was still unsure if it had been panic, or fear that she'd never get the chance, or if the changing feelings she'd been trying to figure out had rushed to the surface to direct her actions, but she had kissed him with no hesitation. She'd kissed him like she meant it, and he'd turned toward her and responded like he'd meant it, too.

Within the space of a few seconds, the air around them changed. The summer had already been too hot, but between them, it was scorching. His hand had ended up behind her neck, bringing her closer to him, and her hands had fisted in his shirt, holding on like the room had shifted underneath her. It kind of had.

Then he'd moved away slowly.

"I have to go. I'm so sorry, Genevieve."

She found out all the details after he'd gone from one of his brother's friends. He'd gotten into mortuary school. Jeremy's dad, and his grandfather, and his great-grandfather, and probably more great-great-greats going back ten or more generations, they were all funeral directors in one of the two Jewish funeral homes in their area. Jeremy didn't like to talk about his family's business, especially after her parents' accident, but it hurt that he'd kept it secret, that he'd shut her out of his life outside of camp. She'd finished the summer without him, then gone to Iceland to finish her dad's sociology research and begin her own postgraduate work.

Real life got in the way of many camp friendships, when distance and other obstacles created boundaries that only disappeared at camp. Deeper, limited-time friendships were normal for kids who spent their summers at Meira, or at any camp, really. There were so many campers who were the best and truest of friends but who only saw one another during the summer. She and Jeremy were like that. Since their first week as campers, through years as counselors-in-training, junior staff, and then senior staff, they'd been best friends. They didn't see each other at all, hardly ever, in the real world. At camp, they were always together.

Then he'd left with barely any warning. She'd finished the summer, then flown away. The following summer, neither of them had been at camp. Gen had still been in Iceland, experiencing the mania that came with unstoppable daylight, and Jeremy hadn't signed on as staff.

They hadn't been together at all since then, for over a year, until now.

At the bottom of her duffel, Gen found the 2013 camp T-shirt and shorts she'd packed. She could wear the T-shirt as a layer beneath six others, but the shorts had no purpose. Still, it had seemed wrong to go to camp without at least one set of Meira clothing, so she'd tossed them in first, before anything else.

She found a place on the shelf for the last of her things and was nearly finished unpacking when Scott poked his head in. "You sure you're okay with staying in this room?"

Gen looked at him. "Yeah, why?"

"It...doesn't have a bed?"

This was true, but she didn't have a lot of options. The bedroom by the back door had no heat and a cracked window besides, and there was no way she'd sleep on the couch in the living room. It was close to the fireplace, but it was also the scene of many staff hookups in years past.

The bedroom she'd chosen had windows that didn't seep cold air, and it had heat. It also had a connecting door to Jeremy's room, but the door could stay closed. All of her problems were easily solved—including the lack of a bed.

"It's fine. I'll go borrow a sleeping bag and air mattress from the OA shack. No big deal."

"I don't want you to be, uh, uncomfortable." There was a wealth of definitions within that one word, none of which Gen was willing to sort through.

"It's fine."

Scott nodded and went back to his room.

When she returned from the Outdoor Adventure shed a few minutes later, the light in Jeremy's room was on, and she peeked inside looking for him. There were piles of clothes, muddy shoes, cross-country ski equipment, and ropes spilling out of a backpack, but no Jeremy. He'd jumped onto the arriving bus to welcome families to Winter Camp, and he must've stayed with them to help unload luggage.

She couldn't even see his bed under all his stuff. He'd arrived right before she had, too. How did he make so much of a mess in so short a time?

Gen went back to her room, tossed the air mattress she'd borrowed onto the floor and unrolled the sleeping bag, causing a flirtatious hint of pot smoke to fill the room.

"Why does it smell like marijuana?"

Scott stood in the doorway, frowning at her.

"Borrowed gear from the outdoor shack," Gen said, looking up at him. "Guess all the heat this fall baked in that fresh pot smell."

"Great." Scott rubbed a hand over his eyes.

"I can wash it." Gen shrugged one shoulder. "And if the smell doesn't come out, we'll roll the sleeping bags into big vinyl doobies and make brownies out of the stuffing."

"Light and airy brownies? Let's do it!" Jeremy's voice carried in from the hall.

Gen laughed. Jeremy stuck his head in the room over Scott's shoulder. "I can has brownies?"

"Nope, sorry."

"Gen, you are cruel. Tempting people with mentions of fine baked goods." Scott backed out of the doorway and Jeremy ducked his head to enter the room. She watched him from the corner of her eye, and when he was within striking distance, Gen pulled a towel out of her bag and snapped it expertly through the air toward him.

"Attacked!" Jeremy feinted to one side and grabbed the towel, pulling it from her hands. "I will defend my honor!"

"Truce!" Gen raised both hands as Jeremy spun the towel into a cord. Instead of trying to snap her with it, he coiled it into a figure eight with flared edges, like an oversized napkin sculpture at a formal restaurant. Then he tossed the bundle back to her.

"So, fair lady. You're making yourself comfortable in the Jiffy Cabin?"

Gen looked around. "Oh, no. Don't tell me you already ripped off the Jiffy Latrine guy."

"Not yet, but he'll be back. And I will be ready." He looked at the adjoining door to his room, then back at Gen. She unzipped her sleeping bag all the way, then shook it to dislodge any potential bugs or pebbles left inside.

"Whoa." He crouched down next to her. "Gen, that really smells like a massive joint."

"Maybe there's one in here," Gen said, inspecting the edge.

"That would be…something." Jeremy grabbed the coiled towel and shook it out. Then he began folding it, flipping one edge over and matching the corners precisely. "Why're you using an air mattress?"

"You see a bed in here?"

"Good point." His ears began to turn red, and he looked down at the folded towel in his hands before he shoved it quickly back into her duffel.

Gen looked closer at the sleeping bag, then sniffed the fabric. "Good grief. Seriously, does no one wash these things?"

"Not really. They're not used for, ahem, *sleeping* after the end of camp, and no one does that laundry until the start of summer."

Jeremy hadn't been at camp this past summer, and neither had she. But he had been on the OA staff the year before, and her imagination picked that moment to torment her with fantasies she'd imagined since then and had tried to forget. Fantasies involving secluded areas in the forest, sleeping bags, and, like he'd said, a distinct lack of sleeping.

Now it was her turn to blush.

"Gross. I turn down sleeping on the nooky couch and end up with the nooky bag." Gen zipped up the fabric and rolled it into a tight bundle. "I have to go back to OA and find another bag that's not crusty, doesn't smell like a joint, and isn't coated with weird stains. That'll be easy."

"Nah, don't worry. I got it." Jeremy stood up and scratched his head with both hands. When he finished, his brown hair stood up in a fuzzy halo around his head, making him seem even taller.

"Nice wolf do."

"Thanks." Then he grinned at her, his face lighting with inspiration. "Follow me, Red Riding Hood, to the storage pit!"

Too small to be a bedroom or an office, the closet at the end of the hall had become a giant pit of random crap over the years. Jer walked toward it, peeking in the other rooms to see if there was anything useful lurking in the empty corners.

Gen followed him. "I can promise you, anything you pull out of the pit is going to smell worse than what I've got already."

"Oh, ye of little imagination."

"I don't need imagination to know that the stuff in there smells."

Jer pulled open the door and looked inside, reaching up to pull the string on the lightbulb and leaning his arm against the door frame above her head. He frowned. "I know I put an old bed frame in here."

"When was that?" Gen ducked under his arm and moved into the closet. Her hand brushed over the softness of his shirt as she slid past him, and she caught a trace of his scent. The familiarity of it made her press her fingers against him, against the firmness beneath the faded cotton of his shirt. It was no big deal to touch him. They hugged, they sat arm in arm by the fire, and they pushed each other in and out of windows in the middle of the night, pulling off pranks that campers still talked about. It should be no problem to touch him now.

Except it was. His shirt and the skin beneath it were very warm, almost hot, probably from lifting luggage and helping families unpack. The muscles beneath her fingers were hard, and there were curves she'd never met before, ridges she wanted to explore and see for herself. He'd changed in the last year and a half—and not just by growing a beard. He seemed more solid, stronger and more at ease with his height and size. He'd never been small, not even as a kid, but when he hit his teenage growth spurt, he'd grown in all directions and kept going. Once they were staff members, he was always the tallest out of everyone, and one of the few people strong enough to move canoes in and out of the dining hall in the middle of the night by himself.

Well, Gen had helped. She hadn't grown much as a teen, so she was small enough for him to lift so she could crawl into windows and unlock doors. She couldn't carry a canoe over her head by herself, but she could help him arrange canoe Stonehenge in the dining hall.

Her hand remained on his side, and though she was looking into the closet, she didn't see any of it. Her attention had been transferred entirely to her fingertips, and they wanted to explore. She yanked her hand away and looked up at him, embarrassed.

He was watching her, a surprised expression on his face. But his eyes were narrow, and his attention felt like she was standing too close to a bonfire.

She moved away, pulling her focus back where it should be. What had they been talking about?

Right. A bed.

Just what she should be thinking about at that moment.

"You put a bed in here? Really? When?"

"About two years ago."

She nodded, turning to face him. "The old wood bed from the cabins down by the lake?"

"Yeah."

"Firewood. Last year. Second session."

"Crap," Jeremy said, one hand in his hair.

"Yeah, it did make crap firewood."

"There has to be a bed somewhere close by that we can move."

"Why? I have an air mattress," she replied.

Jeremy shook his head. "Sleep on the floor? There's, like, icicles down there. Penguins could live in your room. You can't. No way."

She blinked at him.

"Gen. The floor of this cabin isn't well insulated, if at all. There's no way you're sleeping on the floor, and definitely not in a bag that smells like spliff and spooge."

She was trying not to notice the expression on his face, the way he looked at her with concern that made her feel both warm and nervous inside. "Good name for a band," she said.

His grin erased the seriousness. "Totally. See? This is why you're my first choice for partner in crime."

She felt a hot twist in her stomach. "I'm still not helping you steal that sign."

"We can find another sleeping bag." He put one hand on her shoulder and, she noted, ignored what she'd said. He closed the closet door behind them, and his touch brought her with him down the hall. "I have spare blankets in my car, and there are more in the linen supply by housekeeping."

She shrugged. "Okay."

"This is going to be great, Gen. Instead of sneaking out with bug spray, we can stay in and plot world domination."

"Or camp domination. Either way."

He grinned at her, his face happy and relaxed, and she felt guilty for her hesitation around him, her almost instinctive need to push space between them.

"I'm taking this pot-reeking thing back to its pot-reeking friends, and I'll find a less grody sleeping bag on my way back," he said, grabbing the offending coil of fabric and tucking it under his arm.

"Thank you."

"Totally."

She watched him through the window. He marched through the snow, her ex–sleeping bag under his arm. Her smile faded slowly, and she didn't look away until he was out of sight.

Even with separate rooms and a shared door, and no intentions between them, this was not going to be easy.

Gen was folding one of her shirts for the third time when she overheard Scott and his wife, Rebecca, enter the cabin. Rebecca sounded angry.

Gen dropped her shirt on a shelf and went to close her door to give them some flimsy particleboard privacy when she heard Rebecca say, "Yeah, and this time next year you might not have a job."

She froze, waiting to hear Scott's response as they entered their room across the hall.

"I know…" she heard him say, but the rest of his response was muffled when the back door opened. Then the sound of footsteps down the hall covered up everything else. Gen was still holding her breath, wondering if it were possible to hear anything through the walls between her room and Scott's when Jeremy walked in.

"YO!" His voice boomed out, echoing off the walls and ending any audible conversation in the next room. Gen gestured at him to be quiet, then grabbed his arm and pulled him down the hall.

He tried to pull his arm back. "Gen."

Gen held her finger to her lips and dragged him to the back door.

"Genevieve. I just took my coat off and I'm—" He was silenced by Gen's hand over his mouth. His eyes widened.

She stood on her toes and leaned in close, her hand and a fraction of air between their mouths. She saw him glance at her lips, but she didn't remove her hand. She could feel the ice clinging to his beard, and the cold softness of his cheeks beneath her fingertips. His lips twitched beneath her index finger.

"Come with me," she said in a bare whisper, the warmth of her breath covering her hand. "I need to talk to you."

He nodded. She removed her hand, slowly, watching his eyes, but then she lost her nerve and looked away.

Jeremy stood perfectly still as Gen pushed her feet into her boots, put on her parka, and handed him his own, still covered with snow that hadn't melted yet.

"I so do not want to go outside." He spoke on the exhale of his breath, quieter than a whisper, like they'd done so many times sneaking out during the summer. He'd leaned down so his mouth was close to her ear, and when she turned her head to answer, her nose brushed against his. He stood back.

"Just for a second," Gen mouthed at him.

He pointed at two crumpled wads of fabric resting in a puddle. His gloves. The edges were almost steaming as they curled over the front of the baseboard heater.

Gen shook her head at him, then zipped her coat, flipped up the hood, and stepped out onto the back porch. It wasn't much of one, barely big enough to hold the two of them.

He faced her once he closed the door, his mouth drawn into a tight line beneath his whiskers, his eyebrows low over his eyes. "Okay, so tell me: Why do we need to go stand in the snow right now? You needed more cold?"

"Ha. No." Gen was trying to find a place to stand where she could look up into his face and keep her voice quiet, but not so close that she was…too close. She gave up. Jeremy started to push his hands into his pockets, but Gen grabbed his arm and pulled him closer. He stilled the minute she touched him.

"Remember those rumors we heard last year? Before you went home? That camp might close?" Gen whispered, keeping her voice quiet. Her words formed a white cloud and she looked down for a second. She didn't want to see them.

"Yeah. I thought everything went fine this year. I wasn't here, but I didn't hear anything bad."

"I didn't either, but I just overheard Rebecca say something to Scott that maybe next year he wouldn't have a job."

"Oh…shit."

"Yeah."

They stared at each other, no clouds between them. She shivered. Jeremy lifted Gen's hand from his arm and put it into his pocket. His fingers covered hers completely, but she could feel how wet his pocket was, the fleece within soaked like his gloves. What had he been doing, rolling in the snow like a puppy?

Gen shook her head, then tucked their joined hands into her own pocket, which was dry and very warm from being above the heater for so long. Doing so caused him to lean down closer to her, but her hands weren't cold, and his weren't, either.

"What can we do?" Gen asked, staring at precise line of snow on the railing.

"Dunno," he said on a sigh, forming another cloud that blew away from them.

"You think that's why Scott had this crazy idea for a winter camp?"

"Maybe." Jeremy leaned back against the wooden banister. Their hands were still joined, tucked into her pocket, and she allowed herself to be pulled by his movement until she stood next to him, leaning against his arm. "I figured part of it was to prove that the facility had revenue potential in the off-season."

"Can't be much revenue," Gen said, still looking at the snow. "It's got to be expensive to keep the cabins and common areas heated."

"I was just thinking about that." He took a slow breath, and she felt the movement of his body beside hers. "Some of Scott's assignments make more sense now."

"Like what?"

"One of the things I had to do today was hang signs in the cabins. A reminder on each door to turn the heaters down to a lower temperature when the activities are going on."

"You think families will do it?"

"No, but Scott asked me to go around and check that they're set."

"Watching every degree and every penny?"

"Yup. And keeping everyone safe. People put wet stuff on the heaters."

"You don't say." She glanced at him with a smile.

"Plus, there's other little things, like only opening two staff buildings instead of three—and now there's one with broken pipes and a ceiling to fix? Ouch."

Gen felt a tightening sensation in her chest. "Camp can't close," she said, her voice equally tight and strained.

"I agree. Let's think about it and see what we can find out." Jeremy put his other arm around her and pulled her closer, leaning his chin on top of her head the way he always had. The weight of his arm and the scent of his hair were so familiar, she could have closed her eyes and imagined it was summer. But the icy cold of his hand tucked into hers told her it wasn't.

And on the heels of that realization came the awareness of how much had changed. Those changes filled in the space between them, and what had been easy and familiar became stiff and awkward, and she had to move away. Jeremy squeezed her fingers, then pulled his hand out of her pocket. He held the door open for her, and they went back inside without saying a word.

CHAPTER TWO

Tuesday, December 16, 2014—25 Kislev 5775
First night of Hanukkah

Genevieve stood in the back of the group of families gathered around a small table that held an uneven pair of candles. The candles made her eyes burn a little and she resented it, even though she was responsible for them being there at all. That afternoon, as Jeremy was finishing his unpacking, Scott had asked her to find the camp menorah. She hadn't thought there would be such a thing at Meira, it being a summer camp, and had said as much. Jeremy had opened the adjoining door to argue with her, and then he'd gone with her to find it.

Everywhere she'd walked that day, Jeremy had been beside her. It was like déjà vu, only fifty-plus degrees colder.

"Never doubt a Jewish camp has emergency Judaica stashed everywhere. I bet if we needed a menorah, a Torah, and a Jewish statue from Bora-Bora we'd find them in here," Jeremy had said as he'd unlocked the director's summer cabin.

"Bora-Bora? Not very Jewish."

"Could have gone with hora, but I think internationally."

"Yeah. Worldwide, that's you."

"Hey. Don't be calling me wide," Jeremy said over his shoulder as he walked down the hall.

"Wouldn't think of it."

Genevieve resisted looking at his backside, mostly because he was peeking over his shoulder and would see her if she did. She resisted looking again when he bent down to snap the key into the padlock bolted to the floor, and managed to not look to see if his shirt rode up when he stood and reached up to turn on the light.

She slipped past without brushing against his body, knelt in the doorway, and started pulling things off the bottom shelf. She wanted to congratulate herself for her restraint, but it seemed like she was the only one who was hyperaware of the electricity between them, so her ability to avoid contact made her feel worse, not better. Jeremy wandered off into another room, and she figured he had other closets to search, or other buildings to check. There wasn't room for both of them in the doorway.

Sure enough, after digging through boxes and plastic bags, Genevieve found a stash of fat blue and green velvet boxes, the kind that housed items meant for Jewish worship. Most of them were too small to be a menorah—Shabbat candlesticks, maybe. She didn't look inside. But at the bottom of the stack was a big, heavy velvet box, and sure enough, inside was a shiny brass menorah with scrollwork on each arm, etched on every flat surface with vines, leaves, and tiny, tiny flowers.

She picked it up and gasped. The glimpse of her reflection, for a sliver of a second, had looked like her mother's face in the gleaming metal.

"What's wrong?"

Genevieve looked up. She'd thought Jeremy had left.

"You stood around for all that time and didn't help me look?"

Jeremy frowned at her. "I just came back in. Was checking the windows to make sure they were all sealed. It's cold as hell in here."

Genevieve looked down and carefully placed the menorah in the box, wiping away her fingerprints with the sleeve of her fleece pullover.

"Gen. What's wrong?"

"Nothing. It's freezing in here. Let's go." He helped her up, took the box from her hands, and locked the closet again.

Now, a few hours later, showered and changed and wearing nicer, warmer clothing and yet still freezing, Genevieve was looking at that same menorah. It was even shinier than when she'd found it, standing alone on a white tablecloth, tall and beautiful, gleaming beneath two candles. The darkness of the room made the light seem liquid.

She lowered her head so her hair would hide her face. The second anniversary of her parents' deaths had passed on the calendar the week before, but the anniversary on the Jewish calendar was Friday. The Jewish anniversary, the *yahrzeit*, was harder to face. Thinking about it left a dull burn inside her, the way her eyes felt if she stared at the candle flames for too long without blinking.

The prayers went on as Scott led the group in welcoming Hanukkah, saying the blessings and using the tall center taper to light the single candle for the first night. The gentle murmured Hebrew moved around Genevieve like a ghost, and she closed her eyes.

"The light we create does not extinguish, because these traditions came before us, and will last beyond us," Scott was saying.

Genevieve didn't look up from behind her hair, still pretending to study the copied pages that held the prayers and the service Scott had written for the evening. Friday night, the beginning of the *yahrzeit*, would add another year of distance from mourning. Time had moved on, moving her farther from easy memories. She couldn't think back like she had the first year and know her parents had been there: *this time last year, we were making candles. This time last year, we lit the candles. This time last year, we were together.*

Now, looking back a year, she only saw herself. This time last year, she was in Iceland, living in a university dorm with a dozen other students from around the world. This time last year, she and Jeremy had kept in touch online. She'd post pictures of the night skies that never ended, and he'd caption them with typical silliness, all their friends laughing and liking their conversation in an endless visual trail.

She'd traveled so far in literal distance, and in emotional distance, too. For so long it had seemed that memories of her parents would sneak up on her and hit her from behind at odd moments, sometimes for the most inane of reasons. One of her friends in Iceland, a theology student named Sigridur, had called them "grief tackles," and the description was very apt. Now those memories came, but they didn't try to knock her down, or they weren't able to.

When she'd lit the *yahrzeit* candle last year on the first anniversary, she'd been with new friends whose knowledge of her only went back a few months, none of whom were Jewish. She'd been studying the Jewish community of Iceland, which numbered fewer than a hundred people, some of whom didn't want to speak to her about their cultural heritage. Gen looked around the Meira dining hall and realized there were more than three times that many campers at Meira every summer. There were nearly a hundred people in the building right now.

Maybe that was why this year, surrounded by families and people who had known her since she was seven, she felt like she was home. The thought brought tears to her eyes. Not painful tears, but tears of comforted relief. She'd returned from Iceland in late October, and had set up what she thought of as her new life. New apartment, new part-time job at the library, new classes for the spring semester. She'd accepted the invitation to help run Winter Camp partly because she knew she'd have people with her who would understand what she was doing and why when she lit the candle for her parents, and partly because she knew Jeremy would be working, too.

"Hanukkah is a great miracle," Scott continued. He wasn't reading from the paper any longer. "It's made into a bigger deal than it is, liturgically speaking, because of its proximity to Christmas. And, as most kids will agree, there's nothing wrong with presents."

"And fried food," Jeremy said from behind Genevieve. She looked up over her shoulder without thinking, forgetting that her eyes were probably red and her nose was definitely running.

Jeremy glanced at her, then looked again. He'd noticed her tears, and his frowning attention made her cheeks burn.

But he didn't say anything. He stepped close behind her and put one arm around her, his hand across her shoulder, his chin resting on the top of her head.

"You gotta love a holiday like that," he murmured, continuing as if he hadn't noticed she was crying. "Commemorate victory in battle with fried foods? Jelly doughnuts and latkes? It's a beautiful thing."

Genevieve snorted and felt the tears recede. She was tucked into the space between his arms and she felt the warmth of his chest seeping into her skin, chasing the sadness away. She sank past the electric sparks of his touch into the comforting depth of their history together, setting aside the things she wasn't sure of to make room for the many connections between them she never doubted.

His voice vibrated through her when he spoke.

"I know where Scott hid the doughnuts, too," he murmured low into her ear, and she told herself it was the air moving over her skin that made her shiver. "Want to grab one?"

She nodded.

"When we're done, come with me."

She nodded again, but he didn't move away from her.

The collective voices of the families surrounded them as they finished the prayers in Hebrew, and then in English, ending with the blessing over special occasions, said only on the first night of Hanukkah and not the others: *Blessed are you, Lord our God, King of the Universe, who has granted us life, sustained us, and brought us to this day.*

Jeremy's voice was soft, another layer to the warmth of his embrace. Then she felt his lips against her head as he spoke.

"*Amen.* It's doughnut time."

Wednesday, December 17, 2014—25 Kislev 5775

"Make art!"

Twenty heads, some in fleece caps and others in hoods, spun toward him as he stood in the doorway, stomping the snow from his boots and preventing the screen door from slamming against the frame. It looked like most of the kids in camp were there, gathered around the main table, bent over their projects.

"Excellent!" Jeremy continued, his voice muffled bouncing off the gray cinder-block walls as he pulled his balaclava away from his mouth. "Bundled children making art! Have you started making candles?"

"It's all beadwork today, sorry," Gen replied.

"Candles?" A pair of blue eyes above a neon-green fleece scarf looked up at her, then over at Jeremy. "Cool!"

"Agreed, young sir."

Jeremy lowered his voice from the deep bellow that filled the room to a more sedate volume. If he kept it up, he wouldn't be able to talk when he went home.

Then he stopped and looked again. Everyone was wearing coats, hats, and gloves, and he could see their breath in the air above them.

"Gen. Why is there no heat in here?"

"No idea," Gen said, rolling a tiny bead between two fingers as she looked up at him. "Turned it on. Kept turning it up. We're still cold."

"I can fix that." He turned to the group and spread his arms. "Who offers jewelry for heat? I accept bribes!"

No one answered, but he made his way over to the space heater anyway, unzipping his parka and tossing it over an empty chair. He was sweating under his coat, and could feel his T-shirt sticking to his skin. He heard Gen gasp.

"Dude, are you seriously wearing short sleeves? It's below freezing!"

"Yup. Heavy labor this a.m." He'd been moving bunk beds in two of the family cabins, rearranging them so kids who might need to use the bathroom in the middle of the night didn't have to climb down from a top bunk in the dark. Then he'd helped the kitchen staff unload some of the supplies they'd ordered. If he didn't see another fifty-pound bag of flour again in his life, he'd be more than okay with that. He was used to lifting heavy things, but not heavy things that made him sneeze.

He knelt in front of the space heater, which was propped up on two stacked benches, and pried off the cover. Ice coated the heating coils top to bottom.

"Well, this thing's toast. Or the opposite of toast."

"I'll hook you up with jewelry if you can hook us up with heat," Gen replied.

Jeremy smiled at her over his shoulder. Her answering grin was quick, too quick, and she looked down at the project in her hands. He stood up and moved closer to look over her bent head at the green, blue, and silver beads gathered in shiny puddles on the table in front of her. "Hey, nice colors. Like Hanukkah and pine trees."

"Thanks." She gestured with her chin. "Ella picked them out for me."

Jer looked around at the children seated at the table, each building a necklace or bracelet, stringing one bead at a time into a pattern. Some kids had bent the stringing wire back around itself so it looped and coiled in swirls of color, the beads blending into a sweeping pattern. Others were carefully assembling a line of colors that marched in visible order. Ella, who was among the youngest campers, was adding beads to her wire with slow, careful movements, her fingertips peeking out from fingerless fleece gloves. Jeremy strolled down the table looking at all the campers' projects, stopping at Ella's side.

"Whoa, that is some coolness right there. Gen, you see this? Ella has got some serious beadwork skills."

Genevieve hopped off her stool and stood next to Jeremy to take a look. He looked down at her. Well, he looked down at almost everyone he knew aside from his father, but Gen was like a magnet for his attention. Her hair was down again, a long ripple of dark brown curls spilling over her shoulders and across her back. He was so used to seeing it pulled back in a giant ponytail through a ball cap that he'd caught himself staring at her hair several times since she'd arrived. She looked different with her hair down. Older, almost. And her hair was so much longer than he remembered. Had she cut it at all during the time she'd been away?

"Your necklace is way nice, Ella," Gen was saying. Ella's cheeks turned pink, her skin matching the shiny fabric of her parka. "Is that a present?"

Ella nodded but didn't say anything else.

"Gen, you need to get Ella to teach classes in the summer." Several of the older girls overheard and leaned over the table to peek at Ella's design.

"Are you coming to camp next summer?" Ella shrugged in reply to Gen's question, and hunched down farther over her beads.

Jer put his hands on Gen's shoulders, turned her so she faced away from him, and marched her down the length of the table back to her unfinished necklace. He squeezed her shoulders gently before he let go so he could put his coat back on and go find a space heater. Gen looked over her shoulder at him and was about to speak when she froze, her eyes wide, her mouth half-open on an indrawn breath.

She was staring at him. It took him a moment to realize it, because his brain was speeding through every open building, trying to find a space heater he could borrow for a few hours then return before anyone noticed it was missing.

She was looking at where his T-shirt had ridden up over his stomach, and when he absently scratched his chest, her eyes followed his hand.

Was she checking him out?

He felt her gaze like a touch, her attention traveling slowly up from his chest to his neck, his face, and then finally to his eyes.

She was *totally* checking him out.

He felt himself flush, his heart speeding up to push more blood to his face, and elsewhere. He was going to have to take his parka off again. There was probably steam rising off his hair.

Gen blinked and barely smiled at him, a tentative, confused expression he wasn't used to seeing on her face. She looked embarrassed that he'd caught her looking.

He smiled his regular, happy grin. He wasn't embarrassed, but he didn't have a word for how he felt. He moved closer to her, and her head tipped back so she could look up at him. But he didn't say anything.

He tugged one of her curls before heading out to find her some heat. Maybe he could use the space heater in his room. He didn't need any extra warmth—not right now, anyway.

Wednesday, December 17, 2014—26 Kislev 5775
Evening—Maariv, second night of Hanukkah

Later that evening, after sundown, the families were back in their cabins preparing for bed, and he and Gen finally sat down together. Neither of them had anything left on their to-do lists, and they were both exhausted.

"I don't think the activities are working well," Gen said quietly. The light from the fireplace shifted over her as she watched the logs collapse in a shower of sparks. Her dark hair gleamed, the light, like liquid gold, sliding down each curl.

"I don't know, it looked like you guys were having a good time in the art shack."

"We were, but there isn't a lot we can do when it's that cold, even with the space heater—and thank you for that, by the way."

He nodded, watching as she turned to face him as she spoke. They were on the hookup couch, which they'd pushed closer to the fireplace. He was still too warm, though. He had on old, threadbare sweatpants and a T-shirt, but Gen was wearing fleece pajamas over a long-sleeved shirt and leggings, with giant knit socks on her feet. Plus, she was huddled inside one of his hooded sweatshirts, her legs and arms tucked under the hem. It was big on him, but it was so large on her the fabric barely stretched even though most of her was inside it.

"The activities Scott has scheduled are too much like summer camp," she was saying, her voice very low. He stopped watching the curving shadows on her face and listened to her voice. "I mean, I know this is a summer camp, but doing—or trying to do—the same things just…reminds everyone how in the summer it's a lot more fun and a lot less cold. It's not the same."

Jeremy nodded slowly, turning back to the fire for a moment. "Yeah. Trying to mimic summer camp when there's this much snow is not going to convince anyone to get excited about next year. They're going to get excited about going home."

"Exactly."

"So what did you hear during dinner? Anything?" They'd eaten at separate tables, a rare thing for them. They'd each wanted to sit with different board members and try to find out anything they could about Meira and its status for next summer.

"Very little. I sat near the new executive director, Glenn, but he was with his family, so he didn't talk business. Another one of the board members stopped to chat with him, but I didn't hear anything meaningful." Gen rested her chin on what he assumed were her arms, folded inside his sweatshirt. She could use it as a tent in the summer. Then he realized she was waiting for him to speak.

"I talked to some of Nadine's kids in the kitchen—"

"Oh, that was smart," she said.

"I know."

"So modest."

"Always."

Her grin appeared and was gone in a flash, but it moved through him slowly, and he took a breath before he spoke again. "Once Nadine left to go have a smoke, I helped out with the cleaning and started talking to Corey."

"Corey? The one who never talks?"

"He talks. Just not to girls."

"Why?"

"They're scary."

"They're scary?"

"Yes. Girls are scary to Corey."

"*They* are scary? I *am* a girl, you know."

"You're not scary, though."

"Does that mean I'm not a girl?"

"No, you're a mutant. Now hush up and let me talk." Her smile reappeared, and made him feel warmer inside. He might need to change into shorts. No, better if he didn't.

"Go on."

"He said that Nadine has been asking Scott for weeks about when to place the summer food order and what the projected numbers would be, but instead of giving her ballpark figures, he won't give her anything."

"That's not normal. Scott is all about projected figures," Gen whispered. Scott and Rebecca were down the hall, presumably asleep, but neither of them wanted to chance being overheard.

"Yeah, and it gets worse: Corey says his mom's mad about it now. If she can't get a straight answer out of Scott, she's going to look for another job. She won't put her family's summer income on the line for someone who may flake out on her."

"Oh, no."

"It happened to her before. Corey told me. He was with her back when Pine Lake closed. They shut down in late spring with no warning, refunded all the camper deposits and fired all the staff at the last minute."

"I forgot that she came from Pine Lake."

"I don't know how their enrollment declined," Jeremy said. "If she was cooking their food, it would have been some fabulous eating. Woman is a goddess of awesome in the kitchen."

"Yes, and it's totally the food that keeps campers coming back."

"Keeps me coming back."

"Sure, it does. That and all the scary girls."

"Girls aren't scary to me," he said with a grin.

When she didn't reply, he frowned. But she was looking away, into the fire, and didn't see him.

A short while later, she went to bed. Jeremy followed her as far as the doorway to her room, then went to his own. Her voice came through the thin particleboard between their rooms wishing him good night, and he replied just as quietly.

But when he got into bed, the springs on his cot were so loud he jumped in surprise. Then he cursed, louder than he intended. Even his breathing made the bed creak rhythmically, a truly embarrassing sound effect. He heard Gen's laughter, the sound so deceptively close he looked to see if she'd opened their door. It was still closed.

Jeremy spun his sleeping bag and pillow to the other end of the cot and lay down, trying to stay still so his bed would shut up. He watched the thin slice of light beneath the door and the moving shadows that broke it into pieces. She was still awake. The shadows looked like Morse code, a message that maybe she was as restless as he was, and feeling as unsure, and as curious. Maybe she wanted to open that door as much as he did and was just as wary of what waited on the other side. He told himself he wasn't being creepy, watching the lines of her movement in a tiny sliver of light, but he made himself shut his eyes before her light went out.

He was nearly asleep when the door opened, and didn't register that she'd come into his room until her arm on his shoulder woke him up with a start.

"Jeremy?"

"What?" Why was she here? Was something wrong? Did his sleeping bag cover him enough?

"We've got three more nights, right?"

"Here?"

"Yeah."

"Um, yeah. I think so." Math and date identification were not something he could manage at that moment.

"Let's do something."

"What now?" Wide-awake, he leaned up on one arm. Gen sat down on the edge of the bed frame at the same moment, and their movements made the bedsprings squeal. They both held their breath as Jeremy put his hand on her arm to still her, and they waited to see if anyone else was awake. Her eyes were a gleam in the shadows, but it sounded like she was frowning at him when she spoke. He leaned closer to her.

"Say that again?"

"You heard me." The gentle breeze of her whisper moved across his skin, and it was nearly impossible to keep himself from moving even closer.

"You want to...do what?"

"Do something—do something *big*."

"Define, please." He tried to keep his voice level and calm, like he was teaching kids how to climb to the treetops. If he sounded relaxed and confident, they absorbed those same feelings to help them climb. Of course, now he needed to convince himself he was relaxed and confident.

"Let's do something huge, something totally unexpected, and surprise everyone."

Jeremy leaned back down slowly to keep his bedsprings quiet, folding his hands behind his head. It would be freezing and awful to sneak out at night like they usually did, but if she had a plan, he would follow her. "Like what?"

"Not sure—wait, what did you think I meant?"

"Anything, really. Hiring a circus. Landing airplanes on the lake ice…"

"Seriously, listen to me," she whispered, moving her face nearer to his so he could hear her.

"I'm hanging on your every word."

She jabbed him in the ribs with her fist.

"Ow. Go back to your room, wench," he muttered, rubbing his side.

"Listen. What if we did something so spectacular each day for the rest of the week, Winter Camp is the only thing everyone will talk about when they get home?"

"It'll get people excited for summer." He began to understand what she was getting at, though logical thought was nearly impossible with her hip pressing against his.

"We don't have a lot of supplies, or time, and we'd have to do one shopping trip on a serious budget—on our own dime, I bet. And…yeah, Scott would never go for it." Gen stopped, her shoulders slumping.

"No, the two of us can pull something off. We've done it before."

"Can we get away with a trip to the Super Mart?"

"Maybe. But we have plenty of supplies here," Jeremy said. "I just did inventory for this week."

"When did you have time to do that?"

Jeremy shrugged, but he didn't answer.

"So what can we do? Talent shows and stuff like that are already on the schedule. We need something bigger." His eyes fully adjusted to the darkness in his room, and he could see the available light sliding over her skin. She gave him crap for wearing short sleeves but then slept in a tank top? So not fair.

"We need something that makes people look forward to summer but is totally unique to this week. If they start talking about next year..." Jeremy trailed off, mentally thinking through every all-camp activity he'd ever witnessed or run.

Suddenly he leaned up on one elbow again. When the bedsprings rudely announced his movement, he froze, then dropped his voice to a bare whisper.

"Gen, a third of the board is here. If they're thinking of shutting down or selling camp...if we make this week a success, even if it's not a profitable one, it might give them other options to consider."

"Exactly."

"I bet Scott projected this first Winter Camp would be a marginal profit at best, maybe even a loss. But as a vehicle to drive summer enrollment, the risk would be worth it. If they're facing attrition problems, and fewer campers are coming for this summer, then they need new ways to attract campers back as well as bringing in new ones."

"Winter Camp isn't a bad place to start," Gen replied.

Jeremy lay back down, looking up at the ceiling, barely visible in the darkness. "Agreed. If we do something so awesome the campers here talk their friends into coming next summer, that's a successful campaign based on less than a week of activities."

"Exactly. That's why we need something bigger. I mean, the idea of winter camp is great, but Scott's planned activities aren't that special. I don't think the current schedule is going to get people talking at all, except about how cold it is. We need something bigger."

"Yeah. The question is, what *will* get them talking and make camp and Scott and this summer look really, really spectacular?"

The room was silent for a moment, their breathing the only sound. Jeremy closed his eyes to make the darkness complete, berating himself for staring at Genevieve. They'd spent most summers together for years; it wasn't as if he didn't know what she looked like in a tank top. He barely wore a shirt half the summer.

Suddenly, Gen sat up straight, then leaned over and grabbed his arm. He felt her touch everywhere, not just where she made contact. "I've got it."

"What?"

"Color war."

Jeremy stared at her.

"Tomorrow morning, we interrupt Scott, and we break color war. *Winter* color war."

He sat up. Her hand fell away from his skin. "You, my friend, are a fucking genius."

"I know."

"Modest, too."

"Of course."

"Let's go, then." Jeremy reached down over her legs to where he'd tossed his T-shirt. "We've got work to do. Let's get it on."

They worked until nearly two in the morning, facing one another on her sleeping bag with paper spread out around them. Jeremy came up with competitions, games, and team challenges while Gen developed the events schedule. Since his bed squeaked if they so much as breathed funny, they huddled together on her thin camping mattress, even though it wasn't as comfortable. Her room was farther from Scott and Rebecca's, so they were less likely to disturb them, but with both space heaters running, the noise they made was muffled. And he understood why she slept in a tank top, because with both heaters, it was plenty toasty.

Of course, Gen was always cold, so after an hour, she put his hooded sweatshirt on over her tank top. She had to roll the sleeves three or four times to keep them from sliding down over her hands, but he was willing to hide every other warm garment she'd brought if it meant she kept wearing his. His work progress was a little slower than normal, because he kept getting distracted by the curve of her neck when the hood slid sideways over her shoulder, and he wondered what it would be like to kiss her there. But he wouldn't trade the time he lost while staring at her. It had been so long since they'd spent hours whispering plans to one another, he didn't want the sun to rise.

A little after two, they sneaked out to get an enrollment list from the office. Running through the trees in the darkness with Genevieve felt like summer, and yet it was completely different. Gen could barely keep from laughing and kept covering her mouth with her gloves, which made him crack up. Her laughter was contagious.

More snow had started falling, coming down in fat, puffy flakes that covered their tracks within a few minutes. It was cold and scary dark, but he was as happy as he would be on a warm, starry night in mid-July. They were running around at night together, up to no good, as usual.

Jeremy lifted Gen through a window they knew from experience was impossible to lock, and she had the Winter Camp enrollment list in her hand in minutes. They shut the window, hid their footprints with a few stray pine branches and more snow, and headed back to the staff cabin.

"We might need a shopping list. The Super Mart opens at six. We can head out at five if we have to and be there when it opens," Jeremy said, lifting his knees to march through the snow.

"How are we going to start a car without waking anyone?"

"I can get Scott's truck keys from the kitchen. It's parked over by the garbage pickup. No one will hear."

"You scurvy dog."

"We are so doing this, and it will be epic."

Gen jumped in front of his path and threw her arms around him, pinning his hands to his sides. "Stop."

"What?" He jerked once, then went still in her embrace. She'd pressed her body against his, her arms holding tight. She was uphill, so her face was inches from his, her smile wide and bright like a full moon.

"I know you. You're about to throw your arms in the air and holler 'EPIC!' and wake everyone up and knock snow on my head. Not happening."

"You don't know jack." She was right, but he'd never admit it.

"I know you, Jack, and you be quiet. Save the hollering for tomorrow morning."

"Okay. But I know one more thing we're going to need," he said, not moving to break her hold. She stepped away, but he slid an arm around her to bring her near him again and guided her back to the house.

"Caffeine. A boatload of it."

CHAPTER THREE

Thursday, December 18, 2014—26 Kislev 5775

The last words of the morning prayers rose up into the rafters in plumes of white, their collected voices visible in the frigid air. Each person was layered in more down, Gore-tex, and fleece than seemed possible. It was still and sparkling and beautiful in the synagogue pavilion, but it was painfully cold.

"This is nuts," Gen whispered to Jeremy. He watched her out of the corner of his eye. She was huddled in six layers of clothing and was stomping her feet to keep herself warm.

"This was your idea."

"I know," she murmured under a huge yawn. "Why didn't you—"

"Hush—almost time. It's going to be *epic*." He pantomimed raising his arms above his head and yelling. She shook her head.

From their spot on the end of the front row, Jeremy watched Scott climb up onto the stage next to the rabbi. Scott was so bundled in layers he almost tilted side to side as he walked. His arms didn't bend much, either. He had to try twice before he could reach around himself to get into his own pocket.

"Today's schedule is full of activities, so let's get started, shall we?"

The families all sat down amid the shushing sound of nylon against nylon, underscored by the muffled creak of many boots on fresh snow.

"The morning activities are going to start in the—"

Jeremy and Gen unzipped their coats slowly when Scott started droning through his schedule. Then they looked at each other.

He winked at her. Gen smiled back.

"Epic," she whispered.

They drew deep breaths and threw off their winter parkas, revealing shorts, tank tops, and bandannas on their heads. Gen's arms were painted in blue and white stripes. Jeremy ripped his shirt off and pressed a button on the remote hidden in his pocket. Trumpets, drums, and cheering flooded out of the speakers mounted on poles behind them. Everyone in the room flinched back and looked around, including Genevieve. He hadn't told her about the music.

"IT'S COLOR WAR! LET'S GET CRAZY, PEOPLE!" Jeremy bellowed and they leaped onto the stage in front of Scott. Gen grabbed the flags they'd hidden and tossed one to Jeremy as she climbed up the railing. Jeremy stood with his back to her and helped Gen climb onto his shoulders, both of them yelling so loud their voices bounced back from every direction. Music and chaos filled the space where moments before there had been silence and shivering.

Scott's jaw dropped open. The parents gawked. A few birds took off from the rafters and bits of snow fell onto the stage. Then the campers went absolutely wild.

"It's color war?"

"This is *AWESOME*!"

"*YES!* I hope I'm on your team!"

The amount of noise a handful of children were capable of making should never be underestimated, Jeremy thought as campers started cheering and had to be stopped from taking their coats off, too. Their parents gradually got into the fun, standing and cheering until the only person not joining in was Scott.

Jeremy grabbed Gen's knees to hold her still and held on, even though he was more than steady with her weight on his shoulders.

"We're going to announce the teams in just a second," he announced. "Right after Scott goes over the day's activities from the NEW schedule I have here in my very own, very cold hand. The sporting events you are about to hear are now ALL-CAMP COLOR WAR competitions, folks! Get ready!"

Jeremy tried to pass Scott the paper in his hand, but Scott was staring at up Gen, who was shivering in the cold, her lips painted white.

"Yo, Scott, batter up. Time to announce the schedule." Jeremy nudged him with his paper.

"Jeremy, we are so going to have a talk," Scott murmured under his breath.

"Not my idea this time. Talk to the lady upstairs." Jeremy pointed up to Gen, who was laughing and waving at the campers who had rushed the stage to cheer and yell up to her.

Scott turned to the group with a huge grin and shouted, "Are you ready for some color war?"

With red noses and as many tissues as there were flakes on the ground, the winter camp color war teams clomped into the dining hall with snow-covered bodies and huge smiles.

"Silent lunch? Oh, yes, silent lunch!" Jeremy bellowed from his perch on top of the salad bar. His boots were wrapped in garbage bags and his legs dangled over the side like he was sitting on a swing. Gen had no idea how he'd climbed up there.

"Jeremy! Get down off the salad bar!" Scott yelled from the doorway where he was helping his daughter with her coat.

"I'm the king of the WORLD! If the world is made of romaine lettuce and some chickpeas, anyway." Jeremy paused, hands up to his ears. "What's that? No laughing, folks. Any noise is a point deduction from your team."

"That's right!" She'd moved behind him to fill her thermos, and he swung his head around twice before he found her. His exaggerated confused expression made her laugh, along with some of the campers as well. "Oh, no, Jer. Did I hear the blue team start giggling?"

"I dunno, Gen, but you are hereby crowned the judge of silent lunch."

"Hot kosher dog, I am?"

"The power is in your hands. Use it wisely."

"Oh, this is excellent. Thank you, Jeremy, king of the sneeze guard," she said with an exaggerated bow. He nodded at her formally.

"Lady Genevieve, a question?"

"Yes, Your Highness?"

"Do you take bribes?"

"Oh, yes, indeed, I do!" Gen set her thermos on the table, added a tea bag to the hot water within, and stretched dramatically.

"Back hurting, Lady Genevieve?"

Immediately, four campers, two from each team, sprinted to stand behind Gen and massage her back. When a boy named Todd from the blue team reached her first and started rubbing her shoulders, another boy named Seth and his sister, Kelly, each on separate teams, grabbed one of her hands and started warming them.

"Jeremy, I so owe you for this."

A teen camper from the white team went and filled a plate for Gen at the salad bar, taking hints from Jeremy as to which items Gen would like best.

"White team is crafting a big ol' salad for you, Gen," Jer yelled, breaking a silence that held only the sound of eating and whispers. A very carefully assembled salad appeared before Gen, with plastic fork and knife wrapped inside a paper napkin, a white flower made of construction paper holding the bundle closed.

"Excellent presentation, white team! Okay, kids, go eat up. Thank you. Your contributions to my well-being have been noted."

Jeremy added, "Eat lots—it's cold out. And don't forget to tell your parents how silent lunch works!"

The kids scattered, and a low hush of whispers filled the air for a handful of minutes as stunned parents met one another's eyes in shock, then with huge smiles as they collectively realized that silent lunch meant an *entirely silent* lunch. Gen looked up as Jeremy came over with his own plate piled high with salad, schnitzel, potatoes, and bread. "You going to eat all that?"

"Heck, no," Jeremy said in a low voice. "I expect you to bogart half of it. You have to keep warm, too."

"I don't think I have much of an appetite, Jer." Gen rubbed her eyes, which had been stinging all morning. "Too tired. Maybe we're getting too old for the late-night shenanigans."

His eyes widened dramatically, and he covered his mouth with one hand. "Never say that!"

Gen yawned in response.

"Eat, my lady, or pay the penalty."

"Penalty?" Gen unwrapped her fork and speared a potato off the edge of his plate. It was perfect—warm and crispy. Suddenly she was ravenous. She grabbed a schnitzel, two more potatoes, and one of the hunks of bread off his plate, devouring them all in less time than it took Jeremy to finish his salad. "Okay, no penalty required. This is good."

"Nadine. I'm telling you, goddess of awesome. And you can thank me for sharing with you."

"Thank you, Jeremy. The food is awesome and so are you."

"See? People should come here just for the food," he said, cutting his schnitzel into pieces with a plastic fork. "Has nothing to do with the programming or the staff or the *ruach* or any of that other stuff Scott yammers about."

"Oh, really," Scott said from behind Jeremy, smacking him lightly across the back of his head with a rolled-up color war schedule.

Gen grinned at Scott, but kicked Jeremy under the table with her boot.

"Ow," Jeremy said, flicking a potato at Gen.

"I have told you a hundred times, you have the disease," Gen whispered in his ear as Scott headed toward the salad bar for his own lunch.

"Do not. Wait, what disease?"

"The disease where the minute you start talking about someone, they show up behind you."

"I do not."

"Do, too. You got it from me."

Jeremy raised an eyebrow at her. She kicked him again.

"Hey. No kicking. Points off of your team." Theirs were the only voices in the room, and Jeremy was already so loud, his every word echoed in the room.

"I'm on your team, dumbass," Gen muttered.

"What's that you said, Genevieve? You want dessert?" Two campers, one wearing blue and the other in white, sprinted for the dessert table to grab cake, pudding, and whipped cream.

"I'm going to expire from too much sugar and won't fit into my pants. It'll be all your fault, Jer." The campers placed each bowl in front of her, again with a color-coded napkin bundle showing which team had assembled which dessert. "But this looks so good. Thank you."

"You better be sharing that brownie sundae from the blue team." Jeremy reached over with his spoon, but Gen easily blocked his spoon with her own.

"En garde! Do not steal the dessert from the lady of silent lunch!"

"I share my schnitzel and this is how you repay me?"

"You share your schnitzel with all the girls. Don't act like I'm special." Gen pushed his spoon away from her buffet of desserts and kept her expression in place, but inwardly, she wanted to smack herself.

He blinked, jerking back an inch, then he smirked. "You know me better than that. I *never* share my food."

Gen waited for his next move, her spoon inches from his, but when his hand didn't move, she looked at his face. He looked a little hurt, and she felt awful. "You're right. I stand corrected, and apologize deeply to the king of the sneeze guard. But I'm still not sharing my brownie."

"Selfish wench." His smile, warm and intimate, turned his words into a compliment she wanted to savor.

"No, *hungry* wench. My dessert. *Mine.*"

"Fine, I'll get my own."

"What's that, Jer? You like the blue team's brownie sundae?" Gen yelled into the murmuring silence, and four campers made another dash to the dessert table, this time taking a serving platter, filling it with brownies and ice cream, and delivering it to Jeremy with a giant kitchen spoon that Corey gave them through the serving window.

"Now THAT is some dessert right there." Jeremy's smile widened as he counted the brownies in front of him.

"Excellent teamwork. Well played, folks." The campers bowed to the judge and the king and went back to their respective tables, giving each other high fives on way. Then the room fell quiet again, the sounds of cutting, eating, and quiet whispering the only disturbance in the air.

"Darn it," Gen said as she finished the last of her brownie.

"What?"

"Still hungry."

Jeremy moved his plate so she could reach it. "For you, my lady."

Gen smiled, then said in a voice that only reached between them, "I have something for you, too." She reached inside her fleece pullover and pulled out a dry pair of gloves from under her shirt. "Here."

Jeremy took them from her. "Holy sundaes, these are still warm." His cheeks turned dark red as he felt the fabric inside and out.

"I put them in the dryer before I came down to lunch."

"Oh, you are the best. Now your team gets *all* the points, Gen. Thank you."

"I'm *on your team*, Jer."

"Darn right you are," he said with a smile she hadn't seen before, a smile that seemed entirely built out of everything between them that remained unspoken. Then he looked away, stood up and cupped his hands over his mouth.

"Color war teams! Once you have feasted, return to your cabins for rest hour. Then we get our sleds on, and ride the snow to victory!"

The cheers of a handful of families filled the dining hall the same way that 350 campers and staff would during the summer. Gen finished her tea as everyone went from one warm building to several others for an hour of quiet.

Jeremy finished his dessert, eating every bit of the massive platter of brownies and ice cream. Gen watched him over the rim of her thermos as he ate, thinking about his smile.

She knew from last year what his lips felt like, what it had been like to kiss him. But a lot had changed since then, and so much was different, it felt like there were distances between them she didn't know how to cross. He was the same large, loud, effortlessly funny Jeremy she'd always known. But there was something else, too, a sort of quiet stillness that took the place of his almost constant need to fidget and move.

And the beard, she thought as he wiped his face with a napkin. She'd almost not recognized him when she'd arrived at Meira. She couldn't remember everything about the fiery softness of his mouth on hers, but she couldn't forget it, either. What would it be like to kiss him now? Would it be the same?

Her face turned red and then flushed even more when he stood up and pulled on the gloves she'd brought to him. They'd been hidden beneath her shirt, snug against her stomach, and now they covered his hands. But when he helped her on with her own coat and reached out toward her, she put her gloved hand in his and followed him out the door to plan more adventures.

CHAPTER FOUR

Thursday, December 18, 2014—27 Kislev 5775
Third night of Hanukkah

The rest of the day passed in a series of white and blue blurs. There were sledding races and obstacle courses built out of snow and sports equipment, with bridges to cross, tunnels to wiggle through, and flags to collect. Both teams finished the day exhausted, but very happy. The chatter of the room as they gathered for dinner—unfortunately not a silent meal—was more electric and exciting than it had been the night before. Color war made camp more exciting during the summer, and it seemed to have the same effect during the winter, too.

They'd lit the candles for Hanukkah before dinner, saying the blessings together as a group. The first night the group had been quiet and unsure, but that night, as they lit the three candles, it had been difficult to keep everyone quiet. The happiness and energy were so palpable, the flames had danced on the myriad air currents from everyone talking, laughing, and moving closer together.

So far, so good, Genevieve thought to herself. But now the hard part began—setting up one long competition that involved everyone and took up enough hours in the day that she and Jeremy wouldn't need to create additional activities to fill the time before Shabbat prep began.

Jeremy had a few ideas, but in the end, hers had been better. It would be worth the effort, she thought as she followed Jeremy through the late-evening darkness, even if it was going to take nearly the same amount of hours to set up as it would to complete.

And even if Jeremy argued with her the whole time they were working.

"No, listen. What if we dye some of the talcum powder blue?" Jeremy stopped suddenly in the knee-deep snow and prevented her from going around him. She latched onto his parka to keep from falling, and he grabbed her arms. They were trying to keep their tracks as minimal as possible, and if she fell down, that would leave a big, person-sized clue as to where they'd been.

"Let it go, dude."

"But, blue! We could make them blue!"

"No way. The powder wouldn't dry in time. It would be like a paintball battle."

Jeremy's head lifted, his eyes widened, and his smile grew wider.

"No."

He harrumphed loudly, but turned and started marching forward again. He pulled a camp mug he'd taken from the kitchen out of his backpack and stashed it under the bark of a fallen tree. Gen wrote down the GPS coordinates on the device she held. Then they stomped through the snow to another potential hiding spot. Gen looked up, moving her head to see more of the stars peeking from behind the dark branches that tried to hide the endless sky.

"I hope we finish in time, before the snow starts up again," she said, trying to change the subject.

"Me, too. The sky is so clear right now. It doesn't look like a storm's coming at all, despite what Scott said this morning."

After dropping a coil of rope hooked to four carabiners in a hollow tree stump and tucking a spool of neon-green lanyard behind a branch, they marched farther through the forest, Gen close on Jeremy's heels as they headed toward the horse paddock. The sky was barely lit by the moon, and they didn't want to use flashlights. Their plan was to surprise the color war teams with a camp-wide, GPS-enabled scavenger hunt that should take everyone a couple of hours to complete. Not only would it fill time and make everyone, parents and children alike, very tired, but it would show off the GPS equipment that had been donated to Meira and highlight the science programming Scott wanted to develop. Summer sleep-away camps competed with summer learning programs, as Scott had reminded them as he'd handed them each a new handheld GPS unit. Programming that included science and technology made summer camp a more attractive option.

The GPS was so new, there was still a film of plastic on the screen. Gen clutched hers tightly in her hand, afraid of dropping it in the snow and losing it until spring thaw. Scott would kill her.

When they'd left their cabin, everything was so dark, Gen was convinced Jeremy would take four steps away from her and disappear in to the darkness. Now that her eyes had adjusted, the inky blackness had changed into a landscape absent of any color, but it was a landscape she could see. She hadn't fallen down. Yet.

When they reached the edge of the field that held horses in the summer, Jeremy stopped for a moment and rested his arms on the fence, his face looking straight up to the sky.

The stars looked like fragments of glass floating on navy-blue ink, shimmering as wisps of clouds slid above them on the frozen wind. Gen shivered, and Jeremy pulled her closer to him, stepping sideways so his arms were bracketed around her and his body blocked the bite of the air. She faced away from him, but their faces were close, both of their heads tipped way back to try to see the sky all at once.

"I miss the stars when I'm at home," Jeremy said quietly. "It's a lot harder to see them with all the lights from the city. It's not like the sky here."

Gen shook her head. There were very few things at camp that could be reproduced elsewhere.

He glanced at her, then looked up again before he spoke to her. "What?"

"What, what?"

"You're frowning."

"I am? I didn't mean to."

Jeremy looked at her again and raised one brow, but he didn't press her. He waited, but she couldn't find the words to explain how she felt, how she didn't want the camp sky to be the only sky that they saw together. She was still watching him, trying to think of the right thing to say when he looked back up at the stars. Then she spoke fast, without thinking.

"Remember two summers ago, when we were hiking to the waterfall at night?"

He nodded but didn't look down at her.

"And you said that the stars were dead, and the light that was just reaching us was from stars that burned out millions of years ago?"

That made him look at her. "Yeah, I remember."

"That's not…that's not actually true."

"Really?" He shifted back away from her a fraction so he could see her. She had his full attention, and it made heat run through her, warming her from the inside out. He was better than any glove warmer she could buy.

"Yeah. When I was in Iceland, at the school where I stayed, there were a bunch of astronomy students. I called them the star dudes."

"Star dudes?"

"Yeah, a dozen or so. They were doing research on polar astronomy or something. Anyway, one of them told me that most facts about stars posted online aren't true, and that was one of them. I didn't quite fully understand it, but the short version is, the stars we see with our eyes, without telescopes, they aren't dead."

Jeremy's eyebrows dropped a bit, and he moved closer, listening to her. No one listened like him. He paid attention with his whole body, watching and absorbing. He wasn't waiting for his turn to talk. He was waiting to understand everything she said, like she was the center of his orbit in that moment.

"Stars are mortal, like us. They're born, they age, and they die."

Jeremy nodded slowly. That probably sounded very familiar to him.

"But they live longer than we do, like, millions of years longer. Only a few of the stars we can see from the earth without telescopes are actually dying, and astronomers know exactly which ones they are. And they're still a few million years from burning out. They'll die, but not for a long while, long after us."

Jeremy looked up at the sky the same moment she did. When he spoke, his breath formed a faint cloud above her that blew away in the wind.

"So these guys, they're all still alive."

"Yup. They're alive, watching us. Like pervs."

Jeremy laughed, and the sound rolled away from them across the rippled snow, bouncing off the trees beyond and multiplying for a moment before going silent.

"Do you miss Iceland?"

Gen stilled, looking up at the North Star and the glowing clusters she could only see with her peripheral vision. "Sort of. A little, because it was…" She paused. Her time away was all mixed in grief and adventure and research and discovery, and it was difficult to describe.

"It was amazing in many ways, good and bad, but I couldn't live there. I like living here."

"Here? At camp?" They both moved away from the fence at the same time, Jeremy's hands dropping to his sides when she stepped back.

"Ha, I wish." They began their awkward trek through the snow toward the outdoor adventure area where Jeremy planned to hide more items for the hunt.

She did wish she could live at camp, really. Camp was home in a way that nothing else was, and she wished she could live there, that it could be summer all year long, that she could have the friendships that only existed here become permanent parts of her life everywhere.

Gen kept her eyes on the snow in front of her, making sure to step in Jeremy's tracks to keep their trail as small as possible. If they did get the expected amount of snow, their footprints would be mostly filled in, and it wouldn't be obvious where things had been hidden.

"I wish this were my home, too. Sometimes," Jeremy said, pulling himself up onto a low branch and hanging a black leather cord on a loose piece of bark. Gen recorded the GPS coordinates, then looked up at him.

"Not a lot of business here, though," she replied. "Unless you do animal funerals."

"I've done a few," he said, surprising her.

"Really?"

"Yeah, mostly dogs, a few cats."

Gen stared at him. He jumped down from the tree branch and shrugged, looking a little embarrassed, but he didn't start walking.

"We have sample caskets in smaller sizes. Dad doesn't like it, but for most people, pets are part of the family."

Gen nodded.

"But you're right, I couldn't do wildlife. Business would be very slow if I lived here. Not that many Jewish families."

He opened his mouth, like he was about to say something, but then turned and started walking, leaving his unsaid thought behind him. Gen wanted to drag him back and make him keep talking, but she couldn't. It was rare he had something to say that she didn't want to hear, but she'd never been able to make him talk when he didn't want to.

With a shock, she realized that this was one of the very few times they'd ever talked about the real world at camp, that he'd mentioned what he did during the time he wasn't at Meira. She looked at his back and ran a few steps to catch up, wishing she could ask him to say more. Did he want to go into his family's business? Did he live in the apartment above the funeral home? Was he happy there? The way he spoke, the twist of his voice, made her think he was talking about more than funerals.

But she was afraid to ask. And unwilling. She hated people asking her questions about her future, what her plans were. Too many people just asked because they wanted to tell Gen what they thought of her answer, especially now, because everyone who was older than her seemed to think they were some kind of expert on grief. They didn't want to listen. Asking was their way of giving themselves an invitation to talk and deliver their opinion of what she was doing. She'd told him about her frustrations once, and since then, he'd never asked her about anything she was doing unless she brought it up.

But maybe Jeremy didn't mind if she asked. Very few people asked him about his job, or how he was doing, she realized. Maybe because they didn't want to know. It all had something to do with dead people, so unless someone wanted to know about particular funeral details, no one asked Jeremy about how work was going. And if they did, they usually asked in a joking tone, masking their own discomfort. Either way, they never got much of an answer.

"It's always busy," he'd say, his reply identical every time, wry and distant.

But maybe she should ask. She wanted to know what he meant. Maybe he would tell her.

"So…" Gen's voice sounded so heavy and awkward in her ears, she expected to see its tracks in the snow.

"So?"

"Is that why you got your mortuary degree? You're taking over the business?"

He didn't respond right away, and Gen wouldn't have known he'd heard her if she hadn't been watching his feet in the snow. His stride slowed for a moment, as if he was about to stop moving, before he pressed forward again.

"Yeah," he mumbled. "Sort of."

He glanced at her over his shoulder, and as he turned away, she saw him press his lips inward, like he was keeping the rest of his reply in his mouth.

"You can tell me. I won't be upset."

He stopped and turned toward her. "You sure?"

She stepped close to him, his face the only thing in color that she could see.

"I asked, didn't I? I'd...I'd like to know why you went." *Why you didn't tell me why you were going, why I heard about it from someone else.* But she didn't say the rest out loud, as much as she wanted to. This was about him, not her.

He nodded, then started walking, but moved aside and slowed down so she could walk next to him.

"I want to hide some stuff in the supply boxes, because the kids will definitely think to look there." He lifted his chin to gesture to the low ropes course.

"They'll probably look for candy, too."

"I have some," he replied, smiling at her.

"You have candy and you didn't share? You're holding out on me, dude." She shoved her shoulder into his arm. If he'd done that to her, she'd have flown sideways into the snow, but Jeremy hardly wavered as he walked next to her.

He pulled a Jolly Rancher out of his pocket and dropped it into her outstretched glove, then unrolled one for himself. It clicked on his teeth a bit when he spoke.

"I told you Dad wanted Colin to go to mortuary school, right?"

Gen nodded. Jeremy's stories of how different he was from his brother, Colin, were legendary at camp. Colin was the ideal son who did nothing wrong, and Jeremy, well, he figured out the best way to park a golf cart on someone's roof.

"But Colin...he didn't want to. He still doesn't. He doesn't know what he wants to do, but he knows it's not that." Jeremy looked at the long list of items in his hand before he spoke again. "And there's no other way to get a license, really. So I went."

He punctuated his sentence with a shrug, like it was no big deal. But Gen knew he was downplaying his decision. He had mentioned the pressing weight of his dad's expectations one night years ago, back when they were junior counselors. But he'd changed the subject so abruptly that she'd noticed his discomfort, and she'd never asked him about it again. Until now.

"Was it just a year?"

Jeremy shook his head, then jumped over a fallen tree to drop an old baseball glove under a slice of bark.

"Two. I did a year online, then did a year on campus. That part was hard."

Gen marked down their coordinates. "Why? The classwork?"

"No, the courses were mostly good. The ones about counseling and bereavement I liked. I kind of knew most of it, since I've done it already. The finance ones were useful, though my dad won't listen to me on any of that."

Gen watched his face as he spoke. He looked at his list, at the GPS in her hand, at the ground, at the snow in front of them, but not at her. His eyebrows were down, and he was focused, like he was teaching someone how to climb the daredevil pole, one ring at a time on each side.

But he wouldn't look at her. She realized how much she'd held back from him, how much she hadn't said as she recognized how uncomfortable he seemed sharing this part of his life with her. It had hurt that he'd kept all of this from her. But maybe she should have asked sooner. And maybe she should find a way to ask him about everything else that she wondered about, too.

"The on campus stuff was rough because I knew it was a waste of my time. I liked everyone in my classes, and I liked the professors, but it was a huge freaking waste, and that pissed me off."

"Why?"

"Why what? Why did it piss me off?" He stopped to slide an old playing card, an ace of spades, beneath the snow that had collected on one of the supply boxes that marked the start of the low ropes course. He slowly pushed the card sideways with one finger, trying to keep the snow on top from looking as if it had been disturbed. When he stood up and stepped away, the card was completely hidden beneath a pristine shelf of snow.

Gen gave him a thumbs-up before she spoke. "No, why was it a waste?"

He hesitated, then took a slow breath. "I had to learn embalming techniques, cremation, chemistry, stuff that I had to know to apply for a license, but—"

"You'll never use it."

Jeremy shook his head. "Nope. Never."

"How'd you do?"

He glanced at her. "In embalming?"

"Yeah. In all your classes."

He mumbled something.

"What?"

"Got a four point oh."

"Are you *kidding me*?" Genevieve jumped in front of him and punched him in the arm as hard as she could.

"Ow! What was that for?"

"You got perfect grades, you finished your degree with perfect grades, and you didn't *tell* me!"

He rubbed his arm and shook his head at her. "I didn't know you…wanted to know."

Shock ran through her like cold water. He was right. He had no idea she wanted to know about his life because she'd never asked, or let him know that she was curious about him, about what he did in the real world. And of course, with all his training and experience in bereavement, he'd wait before he shared anything with her, out of respect for her own feelings. She felt incredibly stupid, angry at herself for having spent so much time waiting for him to tell her things when she should have just asked him.

She'd opened her mouth to tell him that when she saw his face. She'd been looking at him, but she hadn't really seen him until that moment. He could barely meet her eyes. His eyebrows were down, his ears were turning red, and a deep flush was spreading across his cheeks. He was embarrassed. Very much so. Her anger at herself didn't disappear, but it got out of her way and let her see more clearly.

"I am so proud of you, dude." She reached up, grabbed his neck with one hand, and pulled him toward her. Then she kissed him quickly on the lips, before she lost her nerve.

He stepped back a fraction and blinked a few times before he smiled. "Thanks."

She started walking and he shuffled through the snow behind her. "Did you have to do a final project and all that?"

"Yeah, had to do a thesis, too."

"What'd you write about?"

"Um," he said. Then he coughed and looked down.

"What?" This time she stopped and turned to face him.

He took a deep breath. "I wrote about roadside memorials."

Gen felt the blood leaving her head, the shock that had run through her moments before turning to ice. He stepped closer, reaching out with one hand to touch her arm, but dropped his hand back to his side before he made contact.

Her mouth moved twice before she spoke actual words. "Are they...common?"

He nodded slowly, still watching her. "Very. People want to mark where life ended for the people they love, not just when, or how long it's been."

"Did you write about...?"

"Your parents? No. I wrote about the idea in general, and took some photographs of the memorials that were near the campus."

"I didn't do the memorial for my parents," she said, trying not to picture it in her mind and failing. The plastic flowers, garish pink and orange against the dark brown tree they'd hit—that was all her aunt's doing.

His mouth curved in a half smile. "I know that. Those flowers are fugly."

She laughed quietly and his smile grew a little.

She didn't turn to start walking, though. She watched him, watched his face as he talked about his project, the people he'd interviewed, how some people hated the constant reminders of their mortality, but that others took them as a sign to be careful, and to be grateful.

She couldn't look away.

She wanted to listen like he did, to watch and learn about this person she knew with the curly hair and the big smile, and the person she didn't know, the one with the beard and the purpose. This adult who was sometimes so serious, almost intimidating, but who was also still the guy who always made her laugh.

"You...you like your job," she said, realizing that the look on his face, part intensity and part joy, revealed his contentment.

He stared at her. "I wouldn't do it if I didn't like it. I mean, it's not all good, but I do like what I do."

She cocked her head a bit, waiting for him to say more. He did.

"Life is really short, and I know you know that, and I know that, but sometimes it surprises me. We don't usually get a choice when or where we die most of the time. Before I decided to get my degree and get my license and join my dad full-time, I..." He trailed off and looked up at the stars hiding behind the dark branches. The trees were so thick here that even without leaves, there were very few patches of open sky above them.

"The way I see it, the most important job we have is to make sure we're happy."

Everything she felt for him, that she felt about what he was telling her, how proud she was, overflowed inside her, and she blinked tears away. He was the most amazing person she knew, and she knew him well. But she hadn't known everything about him until she'd asked.

"And if we're not happy, if...I'm not happy, then I have to keep moving toward becoming happy. I have to change what sucks into things that don't suck."

She smiled slowly. "I like that motto. Change what sucks into things that don't suck."

"That's my goal," he said, nodding before he pulled off his cap to rub his hair.

"How many more items do we have on the list? Is your backpack getting lighter?"

He looked down and counted quickly. "About two dozen or so? We should get moving. It's starting to get cloudy."

"Really?" She looked up, but couldn't tell.

They walked a bit before she spoke again. "So what is your job now?"

"With my dad, you mean?"

She nodded, writing down the coordinates as he stashed a few items behind the handholds of the climbing wall. He handed her his backpack and started to climb.

"You're wearing boots, dude. You're going to slip off and fall."

"Nah, I'm not climbing that high," he replied, pulling himself up. His jacket rode up on his back, and his snow pants pulled tight across his hips. She'd seen him in swimsuits and nothing else for days on end, every summer, as long as she could remember, and if the memories made her blush a little, that was probably normal. But now, with multiple base layers and insulated nylon pants, he still had a backside with its own gravitational pull, and she hadn't adjusted to it. It kept knocking her over.

He reached up with a grunt and hid a piece of pottery, a clay Star of David that Gen had made out of scraps, on the edge of a handhold near the middle, just high enough for an adult to grab without climbing too high. Then he jumped down, landing next to her.

"See? Cakewalk."

"Yeah, yeah, you're Spider-Man." She waved her hand at him. "So?"

He shouldered his backpack, shifting the weight on his back while looking at her, his face very close to hers. His eyes were gold and green, but none of the color showed in the dimness. She still knew what they looked like, though.

"Do you..." He wiped his face with one hand, scratching at his beard a moment before speaking again. "Are you really okay with...talking about this?"

She poked him with the cap end of her pen. "Yes. If I didn't want to know, I wouldn't ask. I'm curious." *I want to know more about this different you who is the same but isn't*, she thought, but she didn't say it out loud.

"Okay," he said. "What else do you want to know?"

"What do you like about it?"

"I like the part where I help people figure out what to do when they're lost," he began, leading the way out of the low ropes course and heading for the path to the lake.

"That's not so different from camp." She tucked her pen and paper into her pocket.

"No." He laughed, a short breath of sound. "In one of the classes, I had to write up my résumé, even though I had a job. Speaking of wasted time: half the people there were going into their family businesses, too. No real discussions about inheriting a business and all the things that come with it, but, hey, we all had shiny new résumés with which we did absolutely nothing."

He stopped talking, and when she glanced up, he was looking over his shoulder to see her face. She'd been watching her boots as she navigated the snow and the rocks beneath it on their winding path down to the lake. "Keep talking. I want to know."

He nodded slowly, watching her walk toward him before he spoke. "So I had to do this résumé, and when you've only had a few jobs, that piece of paper is freaking immense. It's like miles and miles of white space to fill in. Paper route? Ha, no. Newspaper delivery *specialist*."

Genevieve laughed. "I didn't know you had a paper route."

"Oh, yeah, when I was, like, twelve. I took over Colin's because he didn't want to get out of bed in the morning."

"So what jobs did you put on your résumé? Did it impress your dad?"

He laughed. "I didn't show it to him. I put camp on there, listing all the jobs I've done here, plus my most excellent paper route, and when I worked as a bouncer."

"You were a bouncer?"

"Yeah. I was big. I mean, I still am big," he said, looking down at himself, like he was making certain he hadn't shrunk unexpectedly. "My friend's cousin had a bar, and even though I wasn't twenty-one yet, she needed some help at the door for a private party, and I looked older than

I was, so I agreed to help out."

"You should have grown the beard then," Gen said without thinking. "Women would have been throwing themselves at you to get in the door."

He looked down at her, eyes widened. She felt her cheeks catch fire, but she didn't look away. She'd meant what she said, and she hoped her smile communicated that fact. She had to be more curious, and be more open and honest, she decided, if she wanted to change their relationship. She had to change what sucked into things that didn't suck, starting now.

"I didn't do it for long, but it was good money for standing around and escorting people out when they got rowdy."

Gen tried to hide her amusement and succeeded only in making a snorting sound.

"What?"

She looked up at him with a grin. "It's your destiny. One way or another, you're showing people the door."

Jeremy started to laugh, which set Genevieve off, and she collapsed against a tree, cracking up into her gloves. She tried to stop, she really did, because she didn't want to encourage him, and they were being loud enough to be overheard from the cabins. But there was no stopping the laughter that rose inside her like a tide, and she clutched the tree behind her to stay upright. Tears ran down her face and her nose ran, and she still kept laughing, pulling herself together for a moment only to lose it again.

Jeremy was no better. He was bent in half, his arm resting against another tree, his eyes tearing. What she'd said wasn't even that funny, but there was so much hilarity built into their history together, it fueled their laughter. He wiped his face with his hat, then took the tissue Gen offered from the pack in her hand.

"Ouch. My head hurts now."

He sniffed. "Yeah, mine, too. Let's finish up. It's starting to get colder."

"Really? I hadn't noticed." Gen looked up at the sky again for any clouds that had sneaked in when they weren't looking. When she turned to Jeremy, he was watching her, a strange expression on his face.

He couldn't look away from Genevieve.

"What?" Her nose was red, and she was scrubbing the moisture from her face, but she'd never looked happier. Or more beautiful.

"Thanks." There was a more behind that one word, but he needed to break it apart to find what he wanted to say.

"For what?" They started down the path, holding on to the bare trees as the trail became steeper toward the lake. Their slow progress gave him time to think.

"For asking."

"I wanted to know. And…like I said. I'm really proud of you."

Her words took up residence in his chest, painful and hot and wonderful, and he took a deep breath to make room for them. "I'm proud of you, too."

"Me? Why?"

He huffed out a laugh. Sometimes she asked some really strange questions.

"You left to go finish your research and traveled really freaking far away, by yourself, when a buttload of people were telling you it was a bad idea."

She waved her hand as if she were brushing them aside. "They didn't know what they were talking about."

"I know that. But I'm glad you didn't listen."

When he didn't hear her footsteps behind him, he stopped to make sure she was okay.

"It wasn't easy," she said as she walked toward him. He waited, half turned to face her on the path.

"I know. But are you glad you went?"

She thought for a moment, coming to a stop right in front of him so when he looked down, her face was the only thing he could see.

"Yeah. I am. No one understood why I wanted to go, why I went."

He waited for her to speak before he started hiking again.

"And people kept asking me what I was going to do, and I could tell they already knew the answer—they just wanted to tell me not to do it. Then I had to be polite when I wanted to scream at them."

"I know. I mean, I know that people didn't get it, and that they told you not to go. But I know why you went. I understand."

He paused to take her hand and help her over a fallen tree before he spoke again, not letting go of her glove. Her fingers curled over his seemed to smooth the jaggedness of her breathing and kept her closer to him, a proximity he never took for granted anymore. "It doesn't always matter if people understand, you know? If you do something that you know is right for you, then who cares what they think. It's your job to find your happiness."

She squeezed his hand. "Right. And change what sucks."

The trail connected to the road down to the lake, and there was enough room for them to walk alongside one another as they made their way to the frozen water. They didn't need to hide their tracks. Enough people had traveled down to the lake and back that the road was covered with boot prints.

"Are you going to travel more?"

"Maybe. I'm not sure."

He looked over at her. Her smile was warm, or maybe it made him feel warm because there was so much pride and contentment in her expression.

"Are you moving back home?"

She looked around. "You mean here?"

He laughed. "I wish. No, back to your old ho—no, wait. You sold it."

"I already did move back. I have an apartment near the university."

"Really? I didn't know that."

"Yeah."

"You graduated, right? I mean—wait, you don't have to answer my questions." He interrupted himself, his hand out in front of him.

She nudged him with her arm, her hand still in his. "It's okay. You can always ask."

"Yeah?"

"Yeah."

He smiled at her, even warmer than before.

"So, yes, I graduated. Earlier this month. I'm starting the PhD program in January, and I've been writing up some of my research in the meantime. I have some interest from magazines who might want some articles about the Jewish communities I studied."

"That's cool."

"And I also have some tentative interest in a book about my travels, but nothing definite."

Jeremy stopped and pulled her to a halt with him. "Are you serious?"

She looked up at him, a confused expression on her face. "Yes?"

"Genevieve. THAT is AWESOME!" His roar echoed off the canopy of branches and probably rolled across the lake ice, too, but he didn't care. "Are you going to do it?"

"Yeah. I'm going to do the articles first, but yeah. I'm going to do it."

He picked her up and hugged her, spinning her around. "I am so proud of you! Holy shit, Gen. A book!"

She looked up at him, her arms on his shoulders then sliding down his chest as he lowered her to the ground. "This isn't a big—"

"Hell YES, it's a big deal. Gen, seriously. That's huge. I—you…" He waved his arms around, unable to fully encompass all the words he couldn't think of. "Seriously. *Dude*."

A grin spread across her face, echoing the monstrous amount of joy in his body. "Dude."

"Dude *indeed*. Can I read it?"

"Read what?"

"Whatever you write? Any of it? All of it?"

"Uh, yeah. Of course."

"Awesome." He put his arm around her shoulder as they walked the rest of the way to the beach. She fit easily in the space beneath his arm, tucked next to his body, and he'd missed having her there for so long that feeling her there made him look repeatedly to make sure she was real.

Then, slowly, she slid her arm around him and hung on. He looked down at where her hand rested on his opposite side, then over at her face. His arm tightened around her for a moment, and he felt the familiarity of her embrace run through him.

He hadn't ever expected to talk to Genevieve about his work, about his mortuary degree, while walking down the road to the lake. That part of his life didn't really belong in his life at camp, his time with Genevieve. He'd never expected to talk to her about any of it, even though he'd wanted to. He'd chickened out last year the night he'd left, and still beat himself up about it. He hadn't known how to tell her that he was going to be a mortician, that he was following his dad into the family business, that he wouldn't be at camp anymore. He hadn't wanted to tell her any of the things about her family, about her parents' funeral.

Ice formed around the warm glow in his chest that had grown in size since she'd started asking him about his degree. He still needed to tell her the rest of it, and he was trying to put together the right words, come up with the right way to explain when she spoke.

"I almost forgot—I have a theme song now."

He took a slow breath. It was easier to rely on the silliness and laughter that lived between them, and he let her change the subject, even though the familiar conversation felt like lying. "It is about time you had your own jam. Everyone needs a theme song."

"I know. This is one of your guiding philosophies."

"It's more than a philosophy." He gestured with the arm that wasn't around her. "It's an absolute rule. So, what is it? No, wait, let me guess."

"Go for it."

Their boots crunched on the crust covering the beach, and the ice collapsed under them immediately to reveal the softer sand beneath. Jeremy kicked at the beach sand with his boot as he thought aloud.

"'Homeward Bound'? No, too cheesy for you. Hmm."

She stood still, tucked into the curve of his arm, against the side of his body, looking up at him as he tugged on his beard and pondered which song she'd chosen. He wanted to kiss her, to feel what it was like to know that he didn't need to leave right afterward, that could kiss her again instead.

Fat, white snowflakes began to fall, and they collected slowly on her hat, in her hair, and around them on the sand.

He had to tell her the rest, he decided, before he kissed her again. If kissing her last year had broken down a boundary between them, it wouldn't be fully erased until he cleared away everything else first. So he looked away and tried to think of a song instead of about sliding his fingers into her hair and kissing her for the next hour.

"Let's see…you were in Iceland. Björk? Jónsi? Something like that?"

"Nope."

"That song about walking five hundred miles?"

"That song gets stuck in my head for days. So, no."

"Great song, though."

"Still not it."

He watched some of the snowflakes as they drifted down from the sky, and even though the air was growing colder, and the wind was more harsh down by the lake, he felt warmer than he had when they started. This was the closeness he missed, that he wanted back. That he wanted to bring home with him.

"Okay," he said with a sigh. "We need to hide the rest of the stuff in my bag and get back before the snow buries us. I give up. But that's the *only* reason—otherwise I'd keep guessing."

"Of course."

"So what is it?"

"I'm not telling you."

"What?"

"Once we hide everything, I'll tell you. When we're on the way back."

"You are a cruel, cruel woman, Genevieve."

"Grab your list—we need to beat the snow."

They hid everything left in his pack and took the more direct route back up to camp. By the time they reached their cabin, the snow looked like it was pouring from the sky. They couldn't see that far in front of them, and their footprints began to disappear almost as soon as they were made.

"We don't have to worry about anyone tracing our steps tomorrow," he said as he took off his coat and hung it over the baseboard heater.

"We might have to worry about whether we can do the scavenger hunt at all," Gen replied, looking at the stream of white through the window. The wind had picked up, and it blew the snow sideways, making him feel as if he were inside a snow globe and someone had shaken it. She looked a little lost as she watched the snow flying by, and he put his hands on her shoulders.

"Fire? S'mores?"

"Jeremy. It's nearly two in the morning."

"So? What's your point?"

She sighed, then shook her head with a half smile. "I'll get my chocolate."

A short time later, they sat in front of the fire, socks pointed toward the flames, trying to quietly munch through crackers and chocolate while licking marshmallow off their fingers.

"So, what's your song?"

"You never forget, do you?"

He looked her in the eyes, the light from the fire shadowing her face. "Nope. Never."

She smiled at him. Her gaze dropped to his lips, then back to his eyes, but that glance made his skin feel as if it were burning. Then her expression changed. "Why didn't you tell me?"

"That's a song?"

"No, why didn't you tell me about…everything?"

"That I'd gotten my degree and all that?"

She nodded, trying, like he was, to eat a hot s'more without making any noise. It was very difficult, but the results were worth it.

"I didn't…" He stopped, trying to find the best way to explain. In the end, he went with the truth. "I didn't think you wanted to know."

She nodded. "I did. And I should have asked."

"I should have told you," he replied quickly. He thought about explaining the rest of what was sitting on his conscience, but the shadows under her eyes made him stop. He'd find a way to tell her, but now wasn't the time. He grinned at her instead. "So? What is it?"

She didn't pretend to misunderstand his question. "Garth Brooks."

"No."

"Yup."

"Really?"

"Yup."

"Which one?"

"It's not obvious?"

He shook his head, the corners of his lips quivering as he tried not to laugh. He took a bite of the last s'more to keep himself quiet.

She sighed. "I changed the words."

"To what?"

"*I Find Jews in Odd Places.*"

His eyes widened, and he nearly choked. He covered his mouth when Gen tried to shush him, a muffled spluttering sound emerging from behind his hand. He rolled onto his back, covering his eyes, shaking his head, and holding in a mouthful of graham cracker and hilarity.

When he lifted his hand to peek over at her, she was smiling at him, with a look in her eyes that was hotter than the fire.

He wanted to answer that look, to meet it halfway across the floorboards and go exploring, but he couldn't. Not right then. He was still unsure, a little off balance with everything they'd talked about, and he didn't want to overwhelm her, or tell her awkward or depressing things before they went to bed…separately.

When he was sure that he could speak without making a mess, he sat up and grabbed the scavenger hunt map off the couch behind him. He saw Genevieve frown briefly, but then she slid closer to him, reaching for her own copies. They went over the schedule, double-checking the items and their coordinates, their heads close together and their muffled voices whispering beneath the crackling of the fire.

74

CHAPTER FIVE

Friday, December 19, 2014—27 Kislev 5775

"Your task, should you choose to accept it, is…"

Jeremy's voice rolled across the snow and echoed off the trees, but when he paused to admire his own reverberation, Gen punched him on the arm.

"Ow! Your task is to build an ugly snow statue of Genevieve!"

Gen pushed aside the weird staccato in her chest when the sound of Jeremy's voice speaking her name echoed across the field.

"Try again."

"Fine. Wench. Your task is to build fine snow statues of your most excellent color war leaders. By which I mean, us. Me and Genevieve. I know that the white team will have no problems capturing my magnificent—OW!"

Some of the kids were laughing with mittens over their mouths. Her own laughter sneaked up and poked at her lips, and she bit them to keep the sound inside.

"You can make Gen however you want. It won't take much snow, since she's—"

"Jeremy!"

"—a perfectly petite person!" He grinned at her, and she glared back.

"This is hardly a fair competition."

"Why not?"

"For one thing, you're twice as tall as I am. They'll need twice as much snow."

"All part of the challenge. They have to make you look majestic next to my own natural…*EPICNESS*."

At his cue, as usual, the campers mimicked Jeremy's arms-up posture and yelled, "Epic!" in return. Gen arched a brow at him.

"Anyway. You all have three hours to build, sculpt, and decorate, and Scott will be the judge. If you need us to pose, we are—*oof*—okay, *I* am more than happy to assist."

Gen rolled her eyes and raised her arms to get everyone's attention. The teams had divided themselves into two groups. One group was in charge of the snow majesty, as Jeremy put it. The other group, which consisted of most of the adults and some of the older kids who were up to a full day trekking through the fresh snow, would be racing on the GPS scavenger hunt.

Gen explained quickly how the hunt worked and handed out the clue sheets, which mixed straightforward GPS coordinates with camp trivia to find plastic flags that would give the teams additional sets of coordinates. As she'd predicted, Scott had been thrilled with the idea of showing off the new equipment and highlighting the programming that would use the same devices during the summer. But she hadn't expected the parental excitement to exceed Scott's. Both teams were eager to go stomping through the forest for hours, digging through the snow for mugs and bits of arts and crafts, and could barely hold still as she explained how the devices worked.

All the kids, especially the youngest campers, were bundled up and showed no signs of feeling cold, or of growing tired of their outdoor activities. That morning, Jeremy had taken the youngest campers on a long snow hike through the woods so the parents could have some time to relax. The campers who hadn't wanted to go hiking were allowed to visit the art shack or do whatever they wanted, as long as they stayed within the camp boundaries. It had been a quiet morning, except for

Gen and Jeremy, who were putting the final touches on the scavenger hunt.

Now that it was time for snow adventures, the fields that marked the starting line and the finish line for the hunt were filled with voices echoing off the trees, laughter and squeals from those hit by snowballs, and the excited and friendly arguments as each team discussed the best route to take to find as many objects as possible for the most number of points.

Gen stood back for a moment and watched. The building teams had started collecting snow to build their sculptures, and the campers teased one another as they rolled bigger and bigger snowballs, eventually making boulders so large that adults had to help push them into position. Jeremy drew a line down the middle of the field by shuffling this boots, marking the areas that would provide snow for each team. When two members of the white team came over to her, she gave them the clothing they'd asked for—her scarf, a pair of mittens, and one of her running shirts. After scrambling through camp late the night before and again early that morning, standing still was a luxury.

Gen took some pictures with the camera of each team as they got started building in the snow, and of the hunting groups as they plotted their route and then ran to get started. When she looked up from the viewfinder, she saw Jeremy looking at her scarf in Ella's hand.

"What?"

He shrugged and grinned at her. "Nothing."

Then Glenn came to stand beside her. Gen was surprised he'd stayed behind. He seemed the type to want to do and experience as much as possible at Meira, especially since he'd only been the executive director for two years, and was still very much the new guy.

"Not doing the scavenger hunt?"

"Nope, not me." He shook his head with a big and genuine smile, not the one Gen had seen him give other members of the board. "Got a bad knee from too much snowboarding out west, so more tromping through the snow would bring too much agony. It does sound like a lot of fun, though."

"I hope so. The clues should take them all over camp."

"You know, Genevieve, you've done a great job with Winter Camp color war. I've seen you and Jeremy running everything, and we're all having a really good time this week. I hope you're coming back to Meira next summer."

Gen looked at him, trying to keep her expression and her tone of voice as neutral as possible. "I hope so, too. If Scott will hire me back." *And if Meira is open next summer.*

Scott, who was talking to Michael, Kelly and Seth's father, overheard and came over to them. Michael, a new member of the board who had gone to Meira himself as a camper and as a counselor, followed Scott. He seemed, in Gen's estimation, to be eager to have any kind of Important Conversation, especially with the camp director and the JCC executive director.

"I hope you'll consider Genevieve for staff this summer," Glenn was saying, still with a genuine smile. Scott's was equally authentic, but Michael's never reached his eyes. "I was just telling her she's done a fantastic job with Winter Camp color war."

"It was Jeremy, too," Gen was quick to point out. "There's no way I could do this by myself. It's as much Jeremy's work as it is mine."

"Yeah, but we both know who does the real work when Jeremy's involved. You need pranks or someone to goof off with, he's perfect. Something like this, we know who really gives the orders." Michael's smile was as slimy as his tone of voice, and Gen wanted to hit him with the GPS she held in her hand.

Scott and Glenn turned to him with shocked expressions. Then Scott spoke in a measured voice. "Jeremy? He might have been when he was younger, but he's a dedicated and valuable staff member now."

Gen had no idea what to say. She knew Michael had been Jeremy's counselor for a summer when they were teenagers, and she knew they hadn't gotten along all that well, but she'd never expected him, or anyone, to trash Jeremy's dedication to the camp, or the work he did as a staff member. She was trying to find the words to defend Jeremy without losing her temper and making a GPS-sized dent in Michael's head when Glenn said with a laugh, "I remember at my summer camp, out in California, I got up to all sorts of trouble. One time we took all the spray cans of room deodorizer that the director ordered and replaced them with spray bait, like hunters use."

Scott's expression was somewhere between horror and amusement.

"So he went to make the office smell like violet springtime or whatever it was, and boom. Everything smelled like rotten shrimp."

Gen had no shame about laughing, but she watched Scott out the corner of her eye. "Don't worry, Scott. No one would ever do anything like that to you."

"No, you just park golf carts on my roof," he replied, shaking his head.

Glenn turned to Genevieve, wide-eyed. "How'd you do that?"

"Trade secrets, sir. Sorry."

"Just tell me this, did you steal the keys?"

"Steal? Oh, no. We hot-wired it."

"I do not want to hear this," Scott said, drawing Michael away from the conversation and steering him toward the snow sculptures that were already beginning to look a little like Genevieve and Jeremy.

When Scott and Michael were out of earshot, Gen took a deep breath and said to Glenn, "He's wrong about Jeremy. I mean, it's not my place to say this at all, but camp is as important to Jeremy as it is to me, and he's not here to make trouble or cause problems."

"Can't hot-wire a golf cart in the snow?"

"We can't even drive it in the snow. Believe me, if we could, we would have." They started walking down the hill toward the staff cabin and the dining hall. "I think we hiked ten miles last night setting up the hunt. A golf cart would have helped a lot."

"Or a snowmobile."

"Yeah. If Scott makes Winter Camp an annual thing, expect a proposal for snowmobiles. From me! I'm tired."

"I imagine you both are. But your hard work has not gone unnoticed, and I want to make sure you know that."

Gen looked up at Glenn, whom she didn't know that well at all, and realized he meant everything he said. She knew Ella, his daughter, from last year at camp, but she hadn't had more than a few conversations with Glenn since he'd arrived to take the job. One of those conversations had been at her parents' funeral, so she barely remembered it.

"Thank you."

"And I mean that for both of you, both you and Jeremy." Glenn paused, pursing his lips, nodding slightly, like he was weighing which words to use. "I know if I went back to my summer camp, half the people there would remember me for the shrimp spray, never mind that it was years ago and I have kids of my own now."

Gen stopped where the path split off toward the staff cabin and looked up at him.

"Sometimes, and I hope I'm not being insensitive, it's easier to be with people who haven't known you all your life than it is to be around people who've watched you grow up and screw up. I'm still the new guy, so I've only met you both as adults. And since I like to think my opinion matters," he said with a laugh, "I say you're both outstanding, and I'm so impressed with what you've done this week."

Gen could feel the heat of pride and embarrassment spreading across her face. It didn't seem fair that they were both going to turn her face red. Pride should be a different color. Like purple or green or something. Instantly she pictured Jeremy, laughing himself silly at the idea of people turning purple when they were proud.

"Thanks. I really appreciate that." Gen shuffled her boots in the snow, unsure of what to do with herself now that she was blushing under the weight of some of the best compliments she'd ever received.

When she returned to the staff cabin a few minutes later, the silence was disorienting, not to mention the fact that she was inside during daylight hours. Gen hadn't paid attention to where Jeremy had gone off to, but he wasn't with her. She had just enough time to get what she needed from the pit closet.

After opening the door, Gen climbed up the shelves on the side of the supply closet, then leaned up to reach the higher shelf above the door. There was a box of old camp T-shirts up there, and she needed them. With one foot on a side shelf and one hand holding onto the wall for balance, she managed to reach the edge of the box. Her plan was to nudge it toward the edge and knock it over onto the floor behind her. She didn't have any extra limbs to lift the box, so shoving it was her best option.

But the box wasn't inclined to move. She climbed up higher onto one of the shelves, but it started to creak when she put her weight on it.

Then Jeremy walked through the doorway, reached up and grabbed her around the waist, scaring the hell out of her.

"What are you doing?"

"Your hands are freezing!"

They spoke over one another and then both fell silent. Gen didn't let go of the shelf above her, so Jeremy moved his hands onto her hips to keep her still, to be ready to support her if she fell, the way he would if they were in the woods on the low ropes course.

That's when the air changed, grew thicker, warmer, as if someone had turned on a space heater and shut the door.

"Ready to let go?" Jeremy said, his voice deeper, rougher than normal.

If she let go, he'd be supporting her weight, lowering her until she reached the ground. She opened her mouth to tell him to step back so she could jump, and felt the air change again.

No, it wasn't the air that changed.

His hands. He'd tightened his grasp on her hips as he stood in front of her, ready to lift her down. She rarely saw him from above. Usually she looked up, but the view looking down was just as fascinating. His biceps were flexed under his T-shirt, and for a split second, she focused on the ragged seam of his sleeve and how tight it was around the curve of his muscles. His shirts were all loose, but that sleeve was almost too small for him.

"Step closer," she said, her voice a dry rasp. She swallowed, then gasped softly as he did as she asked, moving closer to her, placing himself between her legs.

When he nodded that he was ready, like they'd done a thousand times before, she let go. Usually she was sneaking out a window or climbing down a tree, and he'd step back and release her as soon as her feet touched the earth.

This time he didn't let her reach the ground, and Gen wrapped her legs around him so she never got there. Her hands moved to his shoulders, steadying herself against him, and his arms were around her waist, easily holding her against his body.

He scarcely breathed, or blinked. He just looked up at her before reaching up and sliding one hand behind her head as she lowered her mouth to his.

Jeremy could easily think of a few hundred different times that he'd held or lifted Genevieve. He wasn't really twice her height, but she barely reached his shoulder, and if they were breaking into a camp building—maybe one full of golf carts—or into a shed full of canoes, the easiest way in was always for him to lift her up to a window so she could unlock the door.

There were parts of her he'd touched a thousand times, and he only rarely allowed himself to think about them. He'd lifted her or caught her and touched her arms, her sides, her legs. In one memorable misadventure, he'd grabbed her ponytail to keep her from falling against a glass window.

But there were parts of her he'd never touched. Most of her, in fact. He'd touched her waist, but never slid his hands up toward her ribs, and never once had he moved his hands across her back to pull her against him. He'd never felt the soft strength of her body pressed against his own until Tuesday afternoon on the camp road, when he'd pulled her easily into his lap like they were magnets finally turned in the right direction.

Now that he held her tight in his arms again, with her legs around his waist, her breasts pressed against his T-shirt—a flimsy boundary that did nothing to contain his temptation—he wasn't sure his nervous system could handle the experience. Every part of him wanted more of her.

Then she'd kissed him, and his thoughts blew apart into chaos and coalesced into a hot, almost reverent wish for more. He turned and, without meaning to, recreated the position of their first kiss—their first real kiss, one he kept replaying in his mind even when he shouldn't. They'd been in the art shack, the night before he left to go finish his degree certification. She'd been sitting on the high table, and he'd moved closer to her to hug her good-bye, and…he was never sure if it had been an accident, or half an accident that maybe one of them had planned a moment before, but one minute he'd turned his head, and the next they were kissing. He'd been too shocked to move, and then he hadn't wanted to, even though he thought perhaps his hair had caught on fire from the heat between them. When he'd pulled away at the same moment she did, they'd stared at each other. And they'd never spoken of it again.

Now he knew this wasn't an accident, and he didn't want it to be. She was back in his arms in nearly the same position, and he wasn't going to step away or say good-bye. He wanted more. So he turned and lowered her to the edge of a shelf so he could move his hands. She kept her legs around him and pulled him closer, which made him dizzy for a moment. But when he knew she was safe, perched on a plywood shelf with nothing that could hit her head, he allowed himself to find some of the places he'd thought about, but that he'd never touched.

He moved his hands down over her hips. Then his fingertips felt the bare space of skin above her waistband and sought more. He'd put sunscreen on her back many times, but that was brisk, with a normal amount of pressure and the most scientific detachment he could manage at the time. Now, his hands were moving softly over her skin, then sliding with deeper pressure, wanting her closer, wanting to make her shiver, wanting to bring her as much as possible into the space within his arms.

He whispered her name, her full name, in the space between their lips, and she shivered when he spoke. He moved his arms across her back, trying to keep her warm, knowing she was always cold, especially this week. But she moved away, their faces a breath apart. Her eyes were level with his, and he didn't need to tilt his head to see her. Her eyes were wide like his, her breath as quick and uneven as his own. The one time they'd kissed, it hadn't been like this. It had been scary, but enticing, like the first time he bungee jumped or skied down a back-woods powder trail. Thrill and shock and exhilaration before the heat.

Kissing her now felt like dropping into a lit fire, every inch of him combusting at once.

The chill of the room brought her closer, and the sound of his name moved him closer still, and he felt as if crackling flames were deep within his body. Maybe he could breathe fire.

"What are you smiling about," she whispered. She hadn't kissed him again, and he hadn't moved to kiss her, either. They'd been staring at one another, with Jeremy stunned at the intensity between them, the way their closeness had never felt like this.

"I'm amazed I'm not breathing fire right now."

She smiled, then he heard and felt her short laughter as she moved toward him, reaching for him so her hands slid into his hair, her thumbs brushed the thick bristle of his beard. Her lips had just brushed across his when the sound of the back door opening made her stop.

Jeremy stepped back and helped her jump to the floor, and she looked over her clothing, pulling her shirt and sweater smooth. There was no sign that a moment before he'd been about to tear both their shirts and all their base layers off as fast as he could, though it was a good thing his snow pants were loose fitting.

Scott passed them as he walked down the hall, not noticing that they were both in the pit closet. Gen looked up at Jeremy, and the look of shock on her face made him step back away from her. He moved until he felt the shelves on the far wall against his shoulders. He was far enough that he couldn't see the colors in her eyes.

Eventually he found his voice, and a somewhat even method of breathing. "What were you doing in here?"

She frowned at him. He gestured with one hand toward the box above their heads and rubbed through his hair with the other. She looked angry. Was she angry with him?

"Oh, it's nothing. Really."

"You need that box?" He gestured with his chin.

Gen looked up and nodded. "Yeah, it's a little out of my reach."

He laughed, a bare sound with a tension that he could hear and feel. With one hand, he reached up and pulled the box down for her. He tucked it against his side, but she stepped forward and took it from him.

While he could heft it one-handed, she needed to use both arms wrapped across the front to hold it still, a posture that tipped her backward. Jeremy tried to take the box back, but she stepped away and turned toward the door.

"Wait, Gen, I can—"

"No, thanks, Jeremy. I'm good. Thank you, though," she said, her voice thin. He wasn't sure if it was maybe residual breathlessness or the box pressing into her diaphragm. He didn't want her to be unaffected. His own breathing was a mess.

"Wait, Gen, no, seriously." He yanked the cord on the lightbulb and pulled the door closed before he followed her down the hall. "Wait, please. Let me help you."

"I don't need your help," she said, looking up at him. She hadn't spoken viciously, or with any anger in her voice. But her words made him flinch, and she stopped in the doorway to her room.

His mouth opened then closed as he looked at the box, and back at her face.

"See you later?" She moved into her room, hooking her ankle around the door. He nodded, and she smiled at him before she closed the door behind her, leaving him in the hall alone.

Friday, December 19, 2014—28 Kislev 5775
Shabbat—fourth night of Hanukkah

Genevieve had no idea that Jeremy was leading part of that night's Shabbat service. She'd expected to be next to him like she had been during the other services, whispering to him and elbowing him for making her laugh inappropriately. She looked down and allowed her hair to fall over her face for a moment.

She'd wanted him to be next to her.

That night she'd lit the *yahrzeit* candle for her parents, a short, fat candle in a glass jar that would burn for a little over a day. Glenn had lit a second candle with her, in memory of his mother. Ella, his daughter, had held his hand while he did it, and, just for a moment, Ella had leaned her head against Gen's arm, connecting her with their family.

It hadn't hurt as much as she'd expected. Grief was always behind her, Gen thought, and it still tackled her from behind sometimes, but she was moving away from it faster than she realized.

Things that sucked were changing into things that didn't suck so much.

After she lit her *yahrzeit* candle, everyone gathered closer to light the Hanukkah candles. They filled one half of the menorah, and when, last of all, the Shabbat candles were lit, there was so much light, it illuminated everyone's faces as they stood around the table.

She stood amid the crowd of families as they moved through the Sabbath service. She felt the glances in her direction, and if she lifted her eyes from the prayer book, someone was invariably looking over at her, and they'd smile, warmly, with kindness. It wasn't irritating.

But Jeremy wasn't next to her. She'd stood near him for several years' worth of summers, for morning prayer, Shabbat evening services, Shabbat morning, Havdalah, and the prayers before and after the meals. Prayer for her didn't feel complete without the scent of bug spray and pine trees, the sound of the wind in the branches, and Jeremy standing beside her.

That night, he was up front, talking about his hike that morning. He was so animated, his hands and body telling the story along with his voice. He looked like the grown-up version of himself again. Same T-shirt and fleece pullover, same beard and scruffy hair underneath the hat he wore instead of a *kippah*, but he stood straight and proudly tall. He didn't have that languid, goofy restlessness that seemed a permanent part of him during the summer.

"On our snow hike this a.m.," he was saying, "some of the campers talked about what they'd do if they got to lead part of Shabbat services, what they wanted to talk about. So I asked Scott—"

At this, Scott snorted. Apparently asking was not what had happened.

"Okay, I *politely requested—*"

Another snort that turned into coughing, with possibly a muttered denial.

"Okay, fine, I pounded my chest and bellowed across camp that we were taking over part of tonight's service. Kids, you ready?"

From in between parents and behind older siblings, the youngest campers, all under ten, moved forward to the front of the room to stand with Jeremy. A few kids pulled folded pieces of paper from their pockets.

Genevieve watched as some parents stepped back, glancing at each other, folding arms, communicating in many tiny, unmistakable ways that they thought Jeremy wasn't up to the task of leading or of adding anything significant to the evening service. He wasn't the thoughtful one or the wise one. He was one of the wicked children at camp, even as a staff member. They weren't entirely wrong—his pranks and antics with Gen were infamous. They knew he was one who broke the rules and did everything that stood opposite of what he was supposed to do—like surprising the camp director and breaking color war in the middle of a five-day winter camp. Gen wanted to run around and smack their arms down, tell them how wrong they were, but she knew Jeremy could prove or disprove their conclusions on his own.

"While we were walking in the woods, some of the kids were talking about how Hanukkah sometimes felt so much less meaningful than Christmas, and that it stank sometimes that the whole world seems to goes on and on about Christmas, while Hanukkah was like the—what was it?"

Kevin piped up. "Dorky sixth cousin."

"Yeah, that's it—the dorky sixth cousin of Christmas." More parental frowning and muttering slid through the air after that statement, but Jeremy didn't stop talking. "No question that they are a bit related, though. Ella had something to say about that."

Ella stepped forward, a crumpled piece of Jeremy's notebook in her hands, her eyes looking at the paper and not at anywhere or anyone else in the room. Genevieve heard Jeremy murmur something to her but couldn't make out what she said.

Then Ella took a huge breath and said in the loudest voice Genevieve had ever heard her use, "Christmas in the religious sense is about being born, and about being reborn. Christ the baby was born according to the Christmas story, and all Christians are reborn with him in the cycle of his life from birth to his death at Easter."

At this point there was a lot more shuffling and murmuring in the parental audience as the grown-ups grew uncomfortable with the degree to which Christmas and now Jesus were being discussed at a Hanukkah candle-lighting service at the start of Shabbat. Genevieve understood, but she still wanted to smack them.

"But a lot of that gets confusing for everyone," Ella continued, unbothered by the quiet tide of disapproving noises in front of her. "There's so much other stuff about Christmas that the meaning and the significance can get lost behind glitter and lights. If you ask six people about what Christmas means, you'll get a dozen answers and they'll all be different."

Jeremy added, "Just like there's thirty-four different ways to spell *Hanukkah* in Microsoft Word."

Some of the parents laughed at that. Ella tipped her head back and smiled at up him, then looked back at her paper. Her hands were steady, and her voice was strong and clear. Gen felt pride like a warmth rising within her chest, watching Ella speak in front of everyone.

"There are a lot of ways to spell it, and it moves around the calendar a lot, but with Hanukkah, it's always the same. The menorah, the blessing, and the commemoration are always the same. And we can talk about what it's about."

Jeremy nodded. "We talked about this while we hiked up the mountain. Everyone has to answer."

Aniv, one of the youngest campers along with Ella, said, "They tried to kill us. We won. Pass the doughnuts, let's eat?"

The adults laughed more. Genevieve began to suspect that some of the commentary was scripted, but it didn't matter.

Kevin spoke next. "The Maccabees defeated their enemies, and even though they messed up the temple and left everything in a mess—"

"Like your room?" Kevin's twin sister, Kara, asked.

"Yeah, like my room," Kevin replied, elbowing Kara, who smiled and elbowed him back. Their mom had to cover her mouth when she laughed so loudly heads turned.

"The Maccabees took care of the mess, and cleaned up, and even when we didn't think the oil was going to last, we lit the menorah anyway."

"We?" Jeremy asked with a big smile. The parents began to smile as well, stepping forward to make sure they didn't miss a word. A few had pulled out their phones and were quietly taking pictures.

"Yeah, *we*. That's the other thing we talked about. In the synagogue or at home, and during Passover or whatever, everything is *we*." Kevin rubbed the ball cap on his head. "Like we're the Yankees or something."

"Dude. We are so not the Yankees."

Jeremy took off his wool cap and pulled his San Diego Padres hat from his pocket. A wider tide of laughter moved through the group and someone who sounded a lot like Scott yelled, "GO YANKS," from the back of the room. A few heads turned, but just as quickly everyone refocused on the front.

That's right, Genevieve thought, *keep your eyes front where the awesome is happening*. The growing pride that had started when Ella spoke continued to fill her chest as Jeremy encouraged the children with him to say their parts.

"We're on the same team, kind of," Kevin said. "We're the same people who defeated our enemies a boatload of years ago."

A seven-year-old named Sean added, "And Hanukkah is about remembering, too, that as a team we can work together and take care of each other, even when we're outnumbered. And even if we're divided up for color war, we're all on the same team here."

The last child on the end, a girl named Audrey, stepped forward and looked up at Jeremy. He nodded at her.

"So we wanted to say thank you for Winter Camp, and for color war, because we're really glad we all play for the same team: Team Awesome."

"Yeah, Team Awesome!" Jeremy roared with his arms up as the kids cheered and clapped, and the adults joined in with the applause. A few turned around and smiled at Scott, who was making his way to the front with the rabbi to finish services. He shook a lot of hands on his way across the room, and when he got there, his smile was bigger than Jeremy's. He reached over and shook Jeremy's hand before Jeremy took a seat with his hiking group off to the side where there was an empty bench. Gen saw Scott lean over and whisper something else to Jeremy, but she couldn't see his lips to make out what he said.

Whatever it was, he looked happy.

Normally, during summer camp, there wasn't wine—real wine—served for Friday night dinner. But since it was a family week, and since there were more people over the legal age than under, bottles of kosher wine had been added to the kitchen order, and the adults helped themselves.

Genevieve felt strange drinking at camp. Really strange. She was so used to it being forbidden that she felt conspicuous and nervous standing next to Scott and the other staff members holding a plastic cup of red wine. So she drank it a bit too fast, and when the flush of the alcohol spread through her and she finally, finally felt warm, she drank a little more.

After dinner, walking up to the cabin with Jeremy, the cold didn't bother her. She was full of soup and lovely dinner and the sky was cloudy and dark and there were no stars but she wasn't freezing. The wind didn't try to cut her skin like it usually did. Maybe she and the wind could be friends.

She followed the large shadow of Jeremy's back up the hill, through the trees. His footprints in the snow were so large that if she stepped straight into them, no snow fell into the cuffs of her boots, and she stayed dry. Dry and warm.

And she got to watch Jeremy walking. She knew wine was affecting her thinking a little, but it didn't seem like such a bad idea to look at him as much as she wanted. And she wanted. A lot.

It was so dark she couldn't see much of him. The moon was hiding behind low clouds that made everything, even the sound of their breath, more quiet. They hung in the sky, fat and thick, so low she thought she could reach up and touch them. She could barely see the puffs of white each time Jeremy exhaled. Her own breathing was faster than normal. It was a straight-uphill climb to their cabin and it always made her breathless.

The path Jeremy followed took them to the back door, and they left their parkas, boots, and scarves draped over folding chairs and across hooks on the wall so everything would dry by morning.

The absence of any light inside and out made it seem like the middle of the night, except that Gen knew it wasn't much past nine. There were no lights from the city to reflect off the belly of the clouds. There were few lights on at camp, either. It was quiet and still, the loudest sound that of her own heartbeat.

Everything seemed unfamiliar. Even Jeremy seemed unfamiliar. And new.

She watched him rub one hand over his head, ruffling the hair that had been pressed flat beneath his cap as he stepped easily over the puddles on the floor. She had to leap over the cold water and chunks of snow melting around them, and when she jumped toward him, he caught her, one hand on her arm, the other on her waist.

Gen looked up at his face, familiar and different, so similar to the person she'd known for years, so different now that he had a beard and led services and knew what he was doing, and even more different because he'd kissed her, and she'd kissed him.

She looked closer. He had little creases by his mouth that she knew weren't from laughter. Was he stressed out? Was work bothering him? She wanted to reach up and trace the curve near his mouth with one finger. Was she was the reason he looked a little unhappy?

He let go of her without a word, and she followed him to the front room. Within minutes he had a fire going, and she sat on the couch, her heels on the edge of the cushion, her chin resting on her knees. She wasn't drunk, but she wasn't sober. Her thoughts slid into one another like little kids on ice skates.

"Cold?"

She looked up at him and shook her head with a smile. "Thankfully, no. I should drink wine all winter."

He laughed. "Not sure how good for you that would be." Then his face changed and he looked down at the floor for a moment.

"What's wrong?"

"I, uh…I have a candle up here. For you. I know the one you lit earlier is in the dining hall, but I brought one for you. I know you're not supposed to light one after the Shabbat candles, but I thought you'd—"

"A *yahrzeit* candle?"

He nodded. "I thought maybe you'd want one here, too, in the cabin."

"You brought me a candle?"

He nodded again.

She stared at him, and then, slowly, nodded back. "Yes, please. I'd like that."

The candle he brought didn't look so different from the one she'd lit in the dining hall, which would spend the night on the stove, where it could burn all night without any risk of accidental fire. The cabins were different, and she'd have to blow it out before she went to bed, but having the light with her, having a candle that meant he'd thought about how she might feel…it was like he'd brought her blankets and warm socks.

He held the glass in his hand while she lit the candle within, then put his arm around her, holding her against him as the flame moved over the wick and the light grew between them.

"I already said kaddish during services." Her breath stirred the flame as she took the glass in her hands.

"You want to say it again?" His voice was rough and low, but moved over her softly.

She nodded. And when she began the first lines of the mourner's prayer that she knew as intimately as her own breathing, his voice joined hers, their murmured words entwined into one sound that surrounded them both.

He took the candle from her hands and put it on the stone shelf above the fireplace, and then lowered his other arm so that it rested around her shoulders. It took Gen a moment to realize that she'd leaned into him, become almost absorbed into his embrace. The grief she had expected to feel didn't come. Looking up at the flickering light, her head resting on Jeremy's chest, she didn't feel anything but safe, and warm, and curious.

Eventually they moved to the couch, and Gen curled her legs in front of her while Jeremy sprawled out with his feet toward the fire like he usually did. But instead of looking at the flame on the mantel or the fire in the hearth, she watched him. He watched the fire, and she watched his face.

She hadn't had that much wine, but she'd had enough to recognize it was the reason she didn't want to look away. It removed the familiar lines between them and dissolved the boundaries that kept him at arm's length. The wine loosened the division that came with their friendship, but even better, it destroyed the brittle, awkward tension that since they'd kissed had come to rest on their years of familiarity and locked her into patterns of behavior that didn't fit anymore.

"What do we have going on tomorrow?"

"It's Shabbat, so not much," she replied.

"I put some sleds at the top of the hill, so if people want to go sledding, the equipment's already there and no one has to carry it."

"That was good thinking," she replied around a yawn. "A few of the families are more observant than the others."

"And there's late wake-up tomorrow, too." He closed his eyes and tipped his head back against the wood frame of the sofa.

"Best part of Saturday."

He smiled in response, his eyes still closed.

So Gen looked without stopping, without chastising herself, almost without blinking. She didn't want a split second of interruption. The light played over his features, highlighting one, then another. Maybe watching him intently would be like staring at the flames in the fireplace, and his face would appear in the darkness behind her lids when she closed her eyes.

The glints of gold and red in his beard were fascinating, and she stared at his lips, wondering again, was he stressed? Was something bothering him so that the lines near his mouth were tense and deep?

"What?" He looked at her, one brow raised. "Why are you staring at me? Do I have icing on my face?" He ran one hand over his beard, wiping his mouth.

Rushing through the now-absent boundaries that usually held her back, she reached out one hand, and touched his face.

He froze.

Her fingers stroked down his cheek, and she dropped her feet to the floor so she could move toward him. He stayed still, eyes open. She moved closer, stroking her hand over his beard, then into his hair.

His mouth opened, maybe to say something that would stop her, but she stopped him first by kissing him.

A beat, a breath later, he pulled her onto his lap. She fit entirely within his arms, curled across his body. Both her hands were in his hair and she didn't plan to stop kissing him until she no longer needed to breathe. Maybe not even then. Their kiss was fire and heat sliding between them, followed by the overwhelming rush of feeling his lips move over hers. His hands moved across her back, into her hair, pulling her closer so that more of her body touched his. Then he tipped his head and the slant of his lips lit her from within.

His chest, his arms, everything she could reach and touch and feel, was hard and hot. But his clothing, his hair, the way he held her, was soft, and she wanted to run her hands over his skin and explore every contrast, like mapping a trail so she could find her way back.

Then she felt a shock of cold air against her face. He'd moved away. She opened her eyes and saw his look of horror. An even worse burn moved over her face, the shame and flush of humiliation.

"Gen, I..."

She ran her tongue over her lips, tasting him, and she saw him fixate on her mouth. He frowned, a furrow between his eyebrows. Then, dark tension descended over him and she knew he was upset.

She started to climb off his lap, and he let her, but then he took her hand and pulled her toward him so her face was closer to his. She stiffened, unsure.

"Gen, you have no idea, none at all, how much I don't want to stop."

She held her breath.

"But I don't want you to kiss me because you had something to drink. I want you to...because of you."

The burn grew worse, and she was pretty sure her hair was going to turn from brown to bright red any minute. He was right. It was the wine. But also, it *wasn't*. The wine wasn't in her way, or guiding her actions. The wine got her out of her own way.

But before she could explain that to him, he kissed her cheek, close, so close, to her mouth, and whispered good night. Then he stood and went into his room.

A moment later, she heard a small click.

He'd locked the door between their rooms.

The sound of it echoed in her chest until the fire burned down to ashes. She blew out the candle in the jar, went into her room, curled into her sleeping bag with the fabric over her head, and finally, after staring into the black darkness that showed her nothing, she fell asleep.

CHAPTER SIX

Saturday, December 20, 2014—28 Kislev 5775
Shabbat—fourth night of Hanukkah

Saturday morning's late wake-up was perfect for almost everyone. A thin layer of snow had fallen overnight, and clouds remained in the sky. The morning light was dull and easily ignored in favor of an extra hour of sleep.

The staff cabin was quiet when Gen opened her eyes. She knew Scott was probably somewhere else in camp. But Jeremy could sleep through anything, including Scott jumping on his bed to wake him up. Maybe he was still asleep.

After a moment's hesitation, she stood up and tried to open the door between her room and Jeremy's to see if it was still locked.

It wasn't.

But the room was empty. His bed was made, which was weird, and his clothes were piled near his duffel bag, as if he'd made a semi-organized gesture toward the idea of packing.

Gen leaned on the doorway between their rooms, looking at his bag and then over at hers. Packing. They were going home tomorrow.

At camp they were never more than a few hundred feet from one another, but at home, Jeremy lived in the outer suburbs, forty-five minutes or more from where Gen lived now. It wouldn't be so easy to see him after this week. He probably couldn't go so far from his job if he was on call. Did he have on-call hours, even? Probably. She'd have to go visit him. Which would be...

She wasn't sure what it would be. Good and bad, maybe. She didn't like to drive to the town where he lived, where her parents had died.

Gen pulled on another layer, grabbed her hat, and found her boots and coat by the back door, stiff with salt and dirt. She'd have to do epic laundry when she got home. Parkas were a pain to wash, too, if hers even fit in her washing machine.

She didn't want to think about home, about not being at camp, about packing and laundry and saying good-bye. She looked down at the snow beneath her as she walked toward the dining hall. There were no footprints on the path from their cabin, no indication of where Jeremy had gone.

The campers and their parents had a lazy breakfast on their schedules, with cereal, fruit, and bread left out by Corey and Nadine the night before so everyone could help themselves. There was milk in the cooler, and jelly and chocolate spread on the kitchen window counter next to the toaster.

Gen fixed a plate for herself before finding a place to sit. Her breakfast was pretty epic, toast with chocolate on every crumb, and she looked around again for Jeremy. There shouldn't be anything epic going on without him to yell about it.

It seemed that most everyone had lingered after breakfast, gathering around the dining hall fireplace. Wood was stacked nearby to keep the fire going all day. Some had brought knitting or books to read, and others played cards or moved rocking chairs closer to the heat to sit and talk. But there was no sign of Jeremy. It was too quiet for him to be in the room. She'd known as soon as she'd entered that he wasn't there, but she still looked for him.

She stirred her spoon through the milk left in her cereal bowl and tried not to watch the door. Even though she was plenty embarrassed at what had happened the night before, she wanted to find him. Jeremy was one of the most important parts of her life at camp. And she wanted him to be part of her life outside of camp. She didn't know how to make that happen, and she was running out of time in the only place where they had the most time together.

When she stood up to throw her trash away and put her bowl in the dishwashing rack on the counter, she saw a dark figure outside the kitchen windows moving through the trees.

Jeremy.

She ran after him as quickly and quietly as she could, though with the snow it was more of an awkward gallop with a lot of high knees. Jer looked angry and upset. He had his head down, looking at his boots as he hiked quickly away from camp. She watched him and stayed behind, following him without catching up.

The trail he followed, if there was one, took her past the closed sections of camp. The buildings that didn't have heat hid beneath enormous drifts of snow. It was going to be strange to see camp that summer and know that only a few months prior, half the buildings had been buried in white. This was a side of camp that the summer campers would never see, a whole other world that existed by itself. She wanted to say so out loud, but Jeremy was too far ahead and probably didn't know she was there. The way he was looking down, the way his shoulders hunched over, he looked miserable.

She followed him down the path past the kitchen staff's bunkhouses. They were heated, and she could hear music playing as Nadine and her children got ready to head to the kitchens to make lunch.

Jeremy turned into the woods leading out to the tent platforms. The teen campers lived there in the summer, but as she trudged past, Gen saw drifts and lines of snow that were taller than she was, even with her boots on, and possibly taller than Jeremy, too. The winds from the lake were fierce through the trees, and the ridges of snow looked like frozen waves.

She wanted to call his name, to tell him to turn his head and look, but she kept silent again. She had taken the camp digital camera with her that morning, so she took a picture, trying to fit into the tiny camera frame the wide platform that in the summer would be Tent 3, the home of five teenage girls and fifteen tons of clothing and hair product. She could post the picture online later, next to a picture she had taken of Tent 6 last July, to show people how different camp was in the winter.

It was disorienting to see a place that was so familiar look like an alien landscape. She'd probably walked every trail, and seen every part of Meira in the years since her first summer. It seemed impossible that the tent village would change so much in six months. It would be loud, like it was every summer, chaotic with color and noise, with dozens of multicolored towels hanging on the line and tie-dye shirts drying on branches. Now there were silent ridges of snow, white frost layered on black trees, and a wind that whispered as it cut through the village. Nothing looked the same.

There wasn't a path in the snow, but Jeremy's pace didn't slow down, and she had to hurry to keep him in sight once she'd stopped taking pictures. She stayed farther back behind him and let him lead the way through the waist-high drifts and plains of snow. His head was still down, almost defeated, as he continued forward without looking where he was going. He must have known the way because he didn't glance to either side. He didn't take his eyes off his boots as he made deep tracks farther and farther into the woods.

The sounds of camp were already muted in the cold of winter. The slight noises faded behind them, and soon it was only the sounds of their boots crunching on the ground. Jeremy left puffs of breath streaming behind him, like a steamship crossing a white, frozen sea. Gen was short enough that she would pass under the cloud of his breath, her own breathing faster than his.

Jeremy still didn't stop. He kept marching into the woods, following a trail that Gen had never seen in the summer and certainly couldn't see now. She kept her eyes on the ground to keep herself from tripping over a root or a rock hidden beneath the white, and let out a squeak of surprise when she almost fell forward over a log across her path.

Then she looked up and barely stopped herself from squeaking again. Jeremy stood on the other side, expressionless, waiting to help her over the fallen tree. He gave her his hand and held it until she jumped down next to him. Without a word, he continued on his way. He didn't look at her. He didn't speak. His face was turned away from her, and she almost gave up following him, since he didn't seem to want her there.

A beeping noise stopped them both.

"Fuck," Jeremy muttered. He dug into his pants pocket and pulled out his cell phone. He looked at the display and cursed again.

"What's wrong?" He didn't answer her question. "Wow, dude, got serious face?" It was the wrong thing to say. He turned farther away from her.

"Wait, I'm sorry." Gen ran after him. "I'm sorry. I'm not used to seeing you all angry and serious. You look like your dad," she said. Yet again, it was the wrong thing to say. He stepped back, like they were playing dodgeball and he'd forgotten to block a close throw.

"I am...shutting up now. Just...please tell me what's wrong? Are you okay?"

Jeremy leaned back against a tree, almost throwing himself against it, defeat in his every movement. He crossed his arms over his chest, looking down, not meeting her eyes. She could see him pressing his lips together into a thin line, a sure sign that he was angry. Gen refused to let herself speak, to say she was sorry again. She might end up piercing her own tongue with her teeth, but she would give him silence and room to speak.

She'd never seen him like this, withdrawn and serious and still, not a hint of a smile or smirk anywhere near him.

"I have six new messages."

Gen waited. He didn't look up from his phone.

"Something's obviously wrong, but Colin is managing things and he won't call my dad and tell him. He calls me. And then he'll say he tried to reach me but I didn't pick up, and therefore it'll be my fault, because I'm here and not there."

"No one has cell service in camp."

"I know. That's why I walked out here, so I can get a signal. Came out here yesterday and all was quiet. Today? Six messages. He probably messed up something. Or everything."

"Everything?"

"There weren't any funerals, nothing expected. It's not like you can predict them or anything, but it was supposed to be somewhat quiet. He didn't want to cover for me, but he agreed. Now I have to find out what happened, and then tell my dad, and they'll blame me for not being reachable."

"Why?"

"Because I'm here, and not at home, where they think I should be."

"What could he have done wrong?"

"Any number of things."

"What could have happened that he couldn't figure out? What does he...what do you do?"

He looked up, but not at her. His eyebrows were low across his eyes and he stared into the air in front of him.

"If someone died, it would be...pickup and then staying with them. We...I sit with the deceased, or my dad does. Then we make arrangements for bathing and burial preparation." His gaze dropped to the phone in his hand. Gen looked around, saw a tree stump near where Jeremy was leaning but decided not to sit down. She didn't want to move. She didn't know what to say, or what not to say, or what to ask him. But she didn't want him to stop talking.

"Who sat with my parents?" The question was out of her mouth before she could prevent it. She wanted to push it back in. This wasn't about her.

Jer met her eyes for the first time since he'd walked into the woods, and he didn't look away. "I did."

Gen couldn't breathe. "Where was your dad?"

"At the hospital."

"How long?"

He didn't misunderstand her question.

"Two days."

"I was in the hospital for two days."

"I know."

"The funeral was delayed because I wasn't out yet."

"I know."

Gen's eyes began to sting. It was a familiar feeling, but this time it was different, the pain tempered with cold wonder.

"You sat with them. The whole time?"

"Most of it. I took breaks, and people came to relieve me so I could rest, but yeah." He looked down at the snow. When he looked away from her, it felt like something had broken between them, and it made the tears that had burned her eyes start to slide down her cheeks. She felt her scarf begin turn cold and wet but she didn't move to wipe them away.

"You didn't...I mean, you can't eat or drink or sleep when you do that. When you sit with the dead."

"I know." Jeremy's mouth twisted into a wry, sad smile. Of course he knew.

"I can't believe you did that."

"Why not?" He looked up at her again, frowning, his arms still crossed, his phone tight in one hand. He didn't look angry. He looked almost like a stranger again, like someone she didn't know. His eyebrows weren't down, he wasn't smiling, and no part of him was loose or even moving. He was utterly still and serious, almost formal. He looked like an adult, someone far older than her.

"That's why you weren't at their funeral."

"Yeah. Well, no. I could have gone, I wanted to, except…I was sick. Fever. I wanted to go, but I couldn't get out of bed," he said, blinking quickly. Was he clearing tears from his eyes?

Gen was transfixed by this other person lurking inside the guy she'd always known. This serious person beneath the Jeremy everyone saw. She took a half step closer to him, looking up at his face. She'd seen a glimpse of him earlier that week, trying to fix the gate, then again when he'd refused to let her sleep in the bag she'd borrowed and gone to get another one for her. It was like seeing a person she recognized out of the corner of her eye over and over, then meeting them face-to-face. This was who Jeremy became, who he was when they were apart.

"You're so different when you talk about this. Now and when we set up the scavenger hunt. Like Gallant just busted out of Goofus."

He snorted. "Shut up."

"Thank you." Her voice was quiet.

He didn't misunderstand her then, either.

"You are most welcome," he said, in his normal voice. Then his voice changed, grew deeper, more hoarse. "It was my…honor to sit with your parents."

"I didn't…see them."

"I know."

She wanted to ask, but couldn't. He knew. He could tell. He saw her open her mouth to speak, then shut it, then try again. She blinked and tried to come up with the words. She had stepped closer to him, watching him, her eyes narrowed. That pinch of pain between her brows had returned.

So he closed his eyes for a moment and took a deep breath. He didn't want look at her and tell her this part, but he forced his eyes open, forced himself to focus on her.

"Everyone likes to say the dead look like they're sleeping. But that's not…really true. The dead are still, but it's not like sleep. It's more like whatever made them who they were is gone, and the body they had is at peace. It's the complete absence of movement."

Gen took another half step toward him, and he realized he'd turned his face down toward the snow, away from her. So he did what he wanted to do, what he was trying to avoid, and looked at her face. Tears were slowly drawing lines on her cheeks, like a cup just overfull, a few drops escaping over the edge. He reached out and pulled her to him gently, folding her into his arms and leaning down slightly so he could rest his chin on the top of her head.

She fit just like she always did in the space of his arms. He didn't want her to step away, but he was afraid if he told her, if he shared this part of his life, the part that pretty much made up most of his waking hours at home, she wouldn't look at him the same way as she had earlier, with heat and fire and that curiosity that always meant she was up to something. She might not want to look at him at all.

But he didn't want to keep this part to himself anymore. Even if it meant she'd see him and think about her parents, about their deaths, about funerals. Even if it meant she wouldn't see him anymore, he wanted her to know.

"Keep going," she said. He nodded, then cleared his throat.

"You know what happened in the accident, right?" Jeremy asked. Gen shivered, and he understood it wasn't from the cold.

Despite her being one of his closest friends, someone who lived beside him every summer they spent at camp, even with the time that had passed, they'd never talked about it. Not about her parents, not about the accident, not about their funeral, not about any of it.

"Dad skidded on some ice, and we spun, hit a tree." She lifted her head to see his face. "Would you tell me?"

"About what?"

"What happened, why you sat with them? About what you do?"

"Are you sure you want to know?"

She nodded. He pressed his lips together and slowly nodded back. She rested against him, lowering her head to his chest, and he wrapped one arm around her shoulders to keep her warm and close.

"Sitting with the dead is a mitzvah."

"*Shemira*. I know all that. I went to Hebrew school, too. I meant, please tell me what happened with my parents."

"I know what you meant," he said, tightening his arms. "I'm getting there."

She nodded and sniffed, and used her scarf to wipe her cheeks. Jeremy leaned his head back against the tree and closed his eyes.

"One of us keeps watch until it's time for burial."

He was quiet for a moment, turning over different memories in his mind, the quiet of the room where they'd stood watch, all the hours he'd stood and prayed and waited until the next step began.

"I never tell anyone this stuff, and no one in my family talks about it."

"You don't have to—"

"No, I want to tell you, Gen. I want you to know. It's just…hard to explain."

He felt her nod, and felt the movement of her breathing beneath his hands, both inviting him to describe that part of his life.

"Sometimes, if I sit *shemira*, things are unsettled, even in a quiet room where it's just me and the deceased. *Shemira* is standing guard to protect the body, but some scriptures also say that the souls of the deceased stay with their bodies, and the shomer is there is to serve as a comfort. So sometimes I feel like a sort of...guide, to say it's okay to go now."

Gen had a picture in her mind of Jeremy walking through the woods with campers and staff, guiding them on trail hikes and climbing trips. Superimposed on that familiar image was the serious Jeremy who spoke now, quietly guiding the souls of the dead to wherever they were supposed to go.

"Sometimes I pray or recite psalms in my head, but with your parents I was...quiet."

"Why?"

"I couldn't speak."

He took a breath, then another, and found the words he needed to say.

"When your car hit the tree, your dad was killed immediately."

"I know. I was behind my mom, asleep. Lying down on the seat."

"I followed my dad to the hospital to...to get your father's body and bring it back to the funeral home. Then I...your dad, I think...I think his soul had already gone, and when I was with his body, it was quiet. Peaceful."

"Dad did always know exactly where he was going."

"Is that why you never use a GPS?"

"Yeah, I get it from him." Gen blew out a breath that held a fraction of amusement before she stilled. "And my mom?"

Jeremy pressed his teeth together in his mouth, flexing his jaw and trying to keep his voice even.

"I think she..."

"What?" Gen lifted her head and looked at him. Her face was wet, and her expression was so broken, for a moment he couldn't speak.

"You think she...what? Please, tell me."

"I never talk about this," he said, shaking his head. "It's not..."

"I believe you."

Gen stood still though her breaths were jagged, in and out in an irregular rhythm. He kept his arms around her, not wanting to hold her too tightly, but it was easier to speak when he felt her against him.

"I think she waited. Her soul, I mean. My dad came in briefly, but I sat with both your parents that night and...it wasn't like it usually is. It was quiet, but...unsettled."

"Were you scared?"

"No, no, not like that. It's not scary." He shook his head, trying to find the right words. "I think...I think she was waiting and she didn't want to leave. Usually, when I sit *shemira*, it's very still and there's no noise at all. And it's like that in my head, too. My thoughts are...I don't get distracted. It's very focused and peaceful. But with your mom, I couldn't settle my mind."

Jeremy looked down, feeling his cheeks begin to burn, but not just because of the cold. "I was constantly wondering if you were okay, and I was beating myself up about it, because I wasn't supposed to be thinking about myself. I was supposed to be thinking about them. I couldn't stop wondering how you were. No one stopped to tell me and Colin was supposed to relieve me, but he didn't answer his phone and never got my dad's message, so I stayed there."

"For two days."

"My dad and I switched off, but until you woke up, I took every other shift, and I think..."

Gen waited. "You think?"

"I think..." Jeremy lifted his head and looked into her eyes. "I think she was waiting until you were going to be all right, and then she could go."

She stared at him. Afraid to continue but not able to stop, Jeremy went on.

"I remember thinking I wanted you to be okay, that you couldn't die, that there was no way I could sit with you if you did, and no way I'd let anyone else do it. And then, right after I thought that, it was…quiet, like everything smoothed out, and it was peaceful and still again. And that's when I think she went on to be with your dad, because somehow she knew you were all right."

Gen didn't move, and he didn't look away.

"A little while later, my dad came to relieve me, and he told me that you'd woken up." Jer was quiet a minute before he continued. "He told me when he thought the funeral was going to be. That gave me the schedule to prepare, so I got to work."

Gen pressed her lips together, her hands against his chest, her eyes not blinking.

"Then, that night, I felt horrible and went to bed. I woke up the next morning with a high fever, and I couldn't get out of bed. I wanted to go to the funeral, but…" He shook his head. "I didn't finish my job."

Gen shook her head harshly. "Yes, you did. I mean…I couldn't do what you do. Not with people I know, much less people I don't. I…I had no idea."

"That's what I do," he said, like it was his brother's paper route, as easy as biking down a street each morning. "I also do paperwork. Oh, and a spreadsheet. I have, like, nineteen of those. You want to hear about them?"

His smile was gentle and familiar. She laughed, but then it cracked in the middle like ice over the lake, and she broke into gasping pieces. He lifted his hand to touch her hair, and that's when Gen began to cry, taking deep gulping breaths and shuddering as grief and tears and aching sadness took over everything else. Jeremy held her until the air around them was silent and still. Then he held her some more.

Their trek back through the snow took less time than the trip out, even with the time it took Jeremy to clear his voice mail. Colin had lost the password to the office computer, called four times in ten minutes to see if Jeremy would pick up, then called back to say he'd found it—and then again to ask if Jeremy would maybe not tell their dad that he'd lost it.

Instead of following the same trail back, Jeremy took another route, looping behind the tent platforms and heading toward the stables. They passed the ridge that marked the edge of the camp property and moved behind the stables and the paddock. The fields covered with corduroy ripples of snow and the snow statues of each of them were standing guard at the opposite end. Jeremy was quiet while they hiked but kept turning to see if Gen was still with him. With the layers of ice beneath them, it was slow and arduous at points. The winds had pushed the fallen snow across the path they followed, leaving waist-high ridges to climb over or push through. They were breathing heavily and started laughing as they fell into and out of fluffy piles of snow.

Then Jeremy lifted both hands into the air and hollered, "FRESHIES!" before plummeting into a snowbank higher than his head. He disappeared into it and came out covered with clumps of snow clinging to his parka, his hair, even his beard.

Gen laughed until her eyes watered and tried to help him brush the snow off his face, but her gloves did nothing but spread the snow farther, and he swatted her away. She laughed even harder.

Then she removed her glove and with her bare hand began pushing the wet and melting snow from his forehead, his cheeks, his beard, and his mouth. His beard had been trimmed neatly at the start of camp, but it was already becoming scruffy. She liked it either way. She wanted to run her fingers through it, feel it beneath her fingertips, against her mouth, explore the texture for hours, and find out if he was still ticklish beneath his jaw.

She was so intent, she didn't notice that he'd stopped fighting her or pushing her hand away. He'd stopped moving altogether, and when she finally did recognize his stillness, she looked up at his eyes in shock, worried that he was hurt.

Then he smiled. Not his usual giant grin, the one that split his face and encompassed not only himself but the nearest three people as well. It was a small, private smile, one that she realized he only made when she was close to him.

She'd seen it when they broke color war and surprised the hell out of Scott. Scott had been muttering to Jeremy, but Jeremy had looked up at her, and even though a crowd of campers were jumping on her, demanding to know what team they were on, that grin had a gravity all its own, and it had drawn her attention immediately.

Now he wore it again, his eyes green and kind, his smile half-hidden under his snow-matted beard, and she couldn't look away from him, away from his eyes.

She lifted her hands from his cheeks.

"I'm sorry—my hands must be—"

And then he leaned forward and kissed her, and not a chaste kiss, either, quick and absent of possibility. His kiss scorched her, a slant of fire that she needed like she needed air and campfires and s'mores at night. He slowly, gently, brought her closer to him while his mouth melted everything around her.

She didn't want to stop kissing him, and she wouldn't let him pull away, even though their many layers prevented them from getting much closer. When they parted, lips closing and eyes opening at the same moment to look at each other, at first hesitantly and then with warmth and joy, his half smile returned, wider and meant for her alone. Between the fire of his kiss and the welcoming heat of his smile, Gen wanted to take off a layer. Or six.

"We are not done yet, madam," he said, pulling on his glove with his teeth and taking her hand in his own.

"Oh, really?" He started walking and pulled her gently along next to him.

"Our journey continues. Our mission!"

"Oh, no. Is the Jiffy Latrine guy back? Jeremy, we cannot steal that man's sign."

"No, my lady, *you* have a mission."

"I do?"

"Indeed!" She elbowed him and when he glanced down at her, she glared. "Dude. Seriously. Tell me where we're going?"

"No. We journey through the freshies to find your mission!" She elbowed him again, harder. He coughed and tried to hide it with a laugh.

"Fine, most violent one, I'll tell you. When you get up from shivah, you walk around the block."

"I know that. I *did* that, in fact." Going outside and symbolically reentering the world then returning home hadn't been easy. She hadn't wanted to climb up the steps, knowing the house was still empty, that she was the only one coming and going, without anyone to look after her anymore. "But that's after a week. It's been two years."

"And I am aware of that fact, young lady."

"'Young lady'? I'm older than you."

"By two weeks. But I'm taller. And I know things."

She raised one eyebrow. "Like what, that the air is thinner up there?"

He smirked at her, but he didn't speak.

"Jeremy, are you making me hike around camp? That's way unnecessary. And we did that yesterday."

"No, that is not your mission."

"Then what?"

"Trust me," he said, looking down at her, that smile on his face. She nodded, and he didn't speak again until they reached the supply cabin, where all the equipment was stored. He unlocked the door, stepped in, and then jumped out within moments, two ropes, two helmets, and a set of clips in his hand.

"What are you doing?"

"You will see."

He took her hand again, and brought her farther into the forest until he stopped at the base of a pole, a pole that would have looked familiar if there wasn't snow hanging on every nearby tree branch, obscuring it from view until they stood alongside it.

"Wait. Is this the zip line?"

"Indeed, it is."

She shook her head at him as she looked up at the treetops, at the platform above their heads attached to the pole, and the wire attached above it. The snow had been cleared from the platform, and when she looked closer, she saw that the ice and snow had been tamped down around the base so the climbing cleats that stuck out on each side were reachable from the ground.

"What the...?"

"You walk around the block at the end of shiva. At the end of a year, you end mourning. At two years, you fly across the ravine. So it is written."

"What rabbi said that?"

"Rabbi Seatzenpantz."

"Really."

"Yeah. He, uh, flies by the seat of his pants. Pretty popular guy, really."

She looked at the platform, and then at Jeremy, her hands on her hips.

"You made that up."

He looked at her, lowering his chin. "Obviously. But you're going to go zipping." Then he stopped. "If you want to, that is."

She looked up at the cables, which had been reinforced years before to accommodate disabled campers who needed to zip in tandem with a counselor. She hadn't been on the zip line in years, though Jeremy, when he worked at camp, flew across the ravine every day, usually with a camper tethered to his harness.

The warmth that remained inside her from their kiss, from the way he looked at her, spread farther and deeper into her heart, and suddenly, there was almost nothing she wanted more than to fly through freezing air across the ravine on a wire wearing a harness over four layers of clothing.

There was one thing she wanted more.

"Only if you go with me."

His grin might as well have been the summer sun. "I wouldn't miss it. After you, my lady."

She pulled her gloves off, pulled on a helmet, grabbed the harness and clip he offered her, and waited until he had attached both himself and her to the safety lines above them before she put her gloves back on.

"Belay on?" She smiled as she reached for the pole, waiting for him to roar his usual reply. Jeremy liked to remind the ropes course staff that safety resided in attention and in communication. Loud communication. Loud communication that people could hear in the next state.

But this time, his roar didn't bounce off the bare trees or startle any birds.

"On belay," he said softly. She looked over her shoulder. He looked so proud of her, so happy to help her climb, that for a moment, she couldn't move.

"Ready to climb," she said, following the rules.

"Climb on," he replied, and she reached for the first rung, then the second, and the next until moments later she pulled herself onto the platform and grabbed the zip line above her head. The ground looked even farther away than it did in the summer, the monochromatic white and gray disorienting her for a minute. She grabbed the metal bracket above her head and held on.

"Coming up to join me?" She leaned over and watched Jeremy climb the pole so quickly, he might as well have had wings.

"Damn, you're fast."

"Are you insulting my manhood again?"

"Me? Oh, never." He reached up to take the zip line and disconnected her from the safety line that he no longer held.

Then he clipped their harnesses together, looking into the small space between them, focusing intently on the straps and the carabiners, making sure that nothing was twisted, that they were tethered together safely. He tugged on her harness, but not so hard that she lost her balance. She put her hand on his arm nonetheless.

He looked at her, concern and question on his face, his worry over her safety evident in every part of his expression. But when he saw her smile, his face changed, filling with challenge and joy.

"You know that the two of us together won't go as quickly. We won't fly very fast."

"I know." He stood behind her and wrapped one arm around her waist as he clipped them both to the zip line.

"Ready?"

"Ready when you are," she replied. When he jumped, he kept his arm around her. They flew through the air, falling for a brief moment until the zip line caught them and threw them across the ravine, the snow and trees a white blur around them.

Genevieve didn't see any of it. She felt the wind and heard the soft whisper of snow sliding off tree branches beneath the rush of air as they flew. She felt his arms around her, and tasted the biting cold as she breathed in.

The only thing she saw was Jeremy's smile, the one that belonged to her alone, when she tipped her head back to say something, and the words flew out of her mind. He didn't seem to notice they were moving. He watched her face, and when she laughed, he smiled.

She didn't know what would happen when winter camp was over, or what would happen that night. Or the next day.

But for that moment, flying through the cold faster than the wind, it didn't matter too much. The world rushed by them as they flew, but in the space between them she had warmth, and light, and a moment of peace.

CHAPTER SEVEN

Saturday, December 20, 2014—28 Kislev 5775

Despite the thrill of their flight across the ravine, an emotional hangover stayed with Genevieve the rest of the afternoon. It was quiet, and there wasn't much for them to do until dinner, when the team entertainment competition would take place. When they'd hiked back into camp, Jeremy had gone to the kitchen to make sure the cake-decorating supplies were ready, and Gen had gone the other way toward the art shack to spend time on her secret project. It was open, with lanyard and bead supplies left out for anyone who wanted to use them. The artists in charge of each team's sign were putting the finishing touches on their respective plaques, and she'd stayed to help them before they left to go wash up for dinner.

After the arts and crafts shack was cleaned up, all the supplies put away, and the team signs left to dry in the cold air on the porch, Genevieve made the trek up to the cabin to change her clothes for dinner and Havdalah, the service that marked the end of the Sabbath. A path had been cleared to the front door, so she followed that instead of going around to the back.

Jeremy was already inside. She threw her coat on the chair inside the door and collapsed on the couch next to him. The fireplace across from them filled the room with heat and light, and after she pulled off her boots, it nearly set her socks on fire.

"Is every log from the wood pile in there right now?"

"No, but close to it." His voice was flat and low, like he was angry about something.

"What's wrong?"

"Heat in here isn't working too great."

"As in?"

"It's not working in the bedrooms at all."

"And the space heaters?"

"They're not really strong enough. It's pretty freaking cold back there."

"Ooh, boy." Gen closed her eyes. She pictured each building in camp, trying to figure out where there might be extra beds. "Where are we going to sleep?"

"Scott is bunking with his brother's family in their cabin."

"And what about us?"

"I'm sleeping here."

"Here? But your room will be freezing."

"No, *here*, here. Like, in front of the fire."

"Are you going to get up every hour and add more wood?"

"Yup, if I have to." Gen looked at him, baffled. His arms were folded behind his head, and his eyes were closed, his feet propped up on two milk crates, pointed at the fire. The plastic crates were probably melting with the heat.

"Jeremy—"

He turned his head to look at her. "You don't have to stay here—I know you can bunk with one of the families. There are extra beds. But I...I don't want to do that. I have to get up really early, for one thing, and..." He shrugged. "It's easier if I stay here."

He turned back to the fire, watching the flames.

"I'll stay, too," she said softly. Her voice was calm, but her heart was riding white-water rapids through her chest.

He glanced at her, then looked back at the fire. "You sure?"

She nodded, folding her legs under her and leaning her head against the back of the couch, looking at the fireplace. "You have a sleeping bag?"

"Yeah. Got one already."

"Does it smell like a spliff?"

"No, unfortunately."

"That's too bad."

"I did get extra mattresses for us, though. That'll keep us slightly warmer."

"Don't you sleep mostly naked?"

"No. Why, you want me to pitch you a tent?" He looked at her with a smile that was either flirtation or uncertainty.

"Not for sleeping in, no, but thanks." She laughed briefly, then shut her eyes. Suddenly she was so tired, a terrible, familiar weariness like what she remembered from the weeks after the accident. It was partly her own physical exhaustion and partly the deep pool of tiredness that came with grief. Emotional hangovers were almost as bad as alcoholic ones. She didn't feel anything at the moment, no strong emotions that threatened to crash over her. But she was filled with the echoes of how she'd felt earlier, the remnants of sadness that had spun inside her, and the heat that had filled every part of her when he'd kissed her in the woods, leaving the sadness clinging like cobwebs to the corners of a room.

She was tired, confused, and a bit of a mess emotionally. She didn't want to pretend that mess wasn't there by hiding it in a cabin full of people she knew, who'd known her since she was a kid. She wanted to stay here, even if it meant dealing with all those exhausting emotions instead of suppressing them for another night. At least she knew Jeremy would understand them—likely better than she did.

"Are you sure? That you want to stay here, I mean?"

She opened her eyes briefly, and slowly breathed in the scent of him, of the wool of his sweater and the smoke from lighting the fire. Not every feeling he created was exhausting, she realized. Sitting next to him on the couch, she felt desire and contentment and curiosity, none of which were unpleasant.

They'd slept in the same place, in adjoining sleeping bags, before, on campouts and staff retreats. This wouldn't be so different, except that they'd be alone, and they wouldn't have to whisper back and forth after everyone had fallen asleep.

Well, no, they probably still would, but she definitely also planned to kiss him good night. More than once.

"Absolutely."

***

Saturday, December 20, 2014—29 Kislev 5775
Fifth night of Hanukkah

After Shabbat came to an end, with the spice box passed from mitten to glove around the group and the braided candle extinguished with a sizzle in the cup of wine, it was time to light the menorah. Everyone was outside by the bonfire together, waiting for the final team competitions. Scott didn't think they could light the Hanukkah candles outside and keep them lit, so he stood on the porch of the dining hall while the rest of them stood as near as possible to the bonfire without actually being in it.

Gen stood with the firelight in front of her and Jeremy behind, so she felt all of the warmth and none of the cold night wind. When Scott began to shout the blessings so he could be heard over the rattle of the icy branches above them and the crackle of the fire, she felt Jeremy suppress a laugh. She tried to elbow him, but he caught her arm.

When she tipped her head back to smile up at him, the expression on his face stopped her movement, then stopped her breath. He was looking down at her with that secret, almost hidden smile she recognized, but it wasn't just his mouth. His eyes were part of that smile, with the crinkles at the corners and the sunburn on his cheeks. He looked so happy.

Then he slid his arm around her, gently pulling her back against him with his hand across her shoulder. It didn't feel like a friendly embrace. It wasn't unfriendly, but it wasn't just friends, either. It wasn't like the first night of Winter Camp, when they'd stood in a similar position.

Now she was tucked into the space of his arm, and he had pulled her closer to him so that more of her body touched his. If she lowered her chin a fraction of an inch, she could rest her head on his hand, increasing their contact. It made her heart pound, thinking about another part of her touching him, even if it was just her chin and his hand.

A few parents noticed, glancing at them, then glancing away as if the sight of them standing together wasn't really that shocking. Maybe it wasn't. But Gen's chest was a staccato rhythm fueled by surprise and by want. She wanted more of her to touch him, not just now, but later and tomorrow.

The sound of everyone reciting the Hanukkah blessings interrupted her thoughts, and she joined in automatically, the words and recitation increasingly familiar after saying them for five nights. The first night she usually had to think to remember the words, and sometimes the second night, too, but by the middle of Hanukkah, she knew the blessings by heart, and she knew how far the candles would burn down in the time it took to say them.

But this night was different. Jeremy stood closer to her, and it felt like he surrounded her. They'd stood alongside one another nearly every night since they'd arrived, his voice and hers adding to the strange, always identical monotone of people reciting prayer. Now she heard his voice above her head but felt his words against her back, pressing softly into her skin through all the layers she wore.

Did he pray every night, even when it wasn't Hanukkah? He said he prayed while he stood *shemira*. Did he pray at other times?

The warmth of the fire and the sensation of Jeremy's voice against her skin made her face flush, the heat so intense inside and out her skin prickled, and she reached up to rub her gloves against her cheeks. That caught Scott's attention, and when he looked over and saw her, how she was folded into Jeremy's embrace, his arm around her, he frowned. But not at her. He frowned at Jeremy. And Gen could tell by the way he shifted in place that Jeremy saw it.

But he stayed where he was. He didn't step back or move closer. After a moment, Gen lowered her chin to rest on his hand as they finished the blessings and each candle on the menorah was lit.

The final night's bonfire seemed like a good idea—and it had been Scott's idea, too, one that he and Genevieve had agreed with instantly, even before they hatched a plan to turn Winter Camp into a runny-nosed color war. But it was really, really cold, and there wasn't enough wood in the world to make sure everyone there was sufficiently warm.

There were a few final events scheduled, including the team cheer competition and the unveiling of the team signs, which would hang in the dining hall along with the summer camp color war plaques.

Scott made his way over to the bonfire when he was done lighting the menorah, which now sat inside on a table by the window, and held his hands up to the flames to warm them.

"More wood?" Jeremy tightened his arm around Gen for a moment before he let go and moved to add fuel to the fire.

"No, I think we should let it be. We can make s'mores and do the cheers, then move inside for the rest of the evening."

To say there was a sigh of relief would understate the sound that moved through the crowd. It was like the wave at a stadium, only with the crunch of snow under winter boots and emphatic nods and sighs of relief instead of raised arms and yelling.

"All right, then, white team, you ready?" Jeremy's voice reached farther into the darkness around them, but he stopped talking. He could feel his vocal cords getting tired, and his throat was beginning to hurt from the effort. His camp voice was not as strong anymore, because he rarely had reason to use it at home. No one needed shouts loud enough to wake the dead in a funeral home.

The white team began their cheer, a loud, four-part call-and-response with clapping and a rather intricate rhythm pounded out on their parka-covered chests. Gen snapped pictures, focusing in on the kids in the front row and the adults yelling from the back. Jeremy watched her and watched the cheering.

"And what color is the *snow*?" Glenn hollered from the back of the group.

"It's WHITE!" they yelled in unison, throwing tiny snowballs into the air. After a beat of silence, they started clapping, and the blue team applauded as well, showing all the right levels of sportsmanship, a criteria on which both teams were judged.

Jeremy brushed off his hat and tossed snow at Gen as she moved to capture images of the blue team. She ducked and glared at him.

"I'll get you for that."

"Sure you will," he said, laughing. Over her shoulder, he saw Scott glance at him, that frown back on his face. It looked like confusion divided by disapproval.

Then the blue team began. They had props, including stethoscopes from the infirmary and blankets in various shades of blue, and they mimed getting sick from too much cold: "Blue skin? Oh, no. Blue lips? Oh, no, no. Blue team? Oh, YES!"

Gen snapped pictures for the entire performance, and when they finished, she moved to stand beside him.

"Dude. We are in such trouble."

He looked up at her. "Why?"

"Were you not paying attention? Those cheers were excellent."

"Oh, the judging." He thought she'd noticed Scott's frowning.

"Yeah. When everyone's just about done, let's head to the dining hall early and make our decision."

Jeremy nodded, pulling his hat lower over his ears. "I'll grab Scott when everyone's munching, and we'll go convene in the warmth."

In the end, not even the possibility of hot marshmallows and chocolate on graham crackers was enough to entice anyone to stay by the fire longer than needed. Just as Gen, Scott, and Jeremy sat down at the end of a table to check the team standings, which Jeremy kept compiled in his notebook and therefore on his person at all times, both teams came through the doors, licking marshmallow and chocolate off their fingers and moving to the fireplace as fast as possible.

"Well, then." Scott had to raise his voice over the increased noise in the room, and it looked like it hurt a little. "Let's do the sign presentation, and I'll make announcements about packing up and bus arrival for tomorrow while you guys do quick math."

"I have some stuff to present, too—so, Jeremy, can you handle the total?"

"The total? Totally," he said, grinning widely. "What are you presenting?"

Before she left the table, Jeremy tapped her arm. "Wait. Do you have your phone?"

"Of course, why?" It was her watch, her alarm, her schedule, and her emergency camera, so she kept her phone with her even if it didn't work in camp as an actual telephone.

"You have a calculator."

"You don't?" He didn't answer, just held out his hand and waited. Gen shook her head, handed her phone over, and then carried the team plaques, covered in old tie-dyed sheets, over to the fireplace.

Scott was finishing up whatever announcements he'd decided to make, or had made up on the spot, and turned to Gen. "Ready to show off the team signs?"

Jeremy checked his work from earlier, adding the afternoon scores to the tally, but before he could add the points for team cheers, the sound of Gen's voice stopped him. She'd asked the team artists to come forward to present their team plaques, and there were flashes from cameras and cheering and applause for each one.

The dining hall was a long, rectangular building with the kitchen on one end and the large fireplace at the other. But since the beginning of Winter Camp, the dining hall and every other room where Gen was present had seemed round, with her as the axis around which everyone turned. She was the center of every room for him, and he had a hard time looking away.

She was taking pictures, smiling and laughing, arranging the teams behind their signs for group pictures, teasing the adults who didn't smile. She looked so content, and the rhythm of the room seemed to flow around her, the movement of people and voices circling back while he watched, like she was the heart of everything.

When Jeremy tuned back in to what was being said, Scott was showing everyone where they'd be hung that summer.

"Above the fireplace," Ella called out.

"It was Winter Camp," Scott agreed with a smile. "You spent most of your time here."

Then Glenn stood, his posture formal, and asked if he could say a few words. Jeremy snorted to himself. Like Scott would ever say to the executive director, "No, no, person who is my boss, you can't talk."

Fortunately, Glenn wasn't into long, wandering speeches.

"I want to start by saying thank you to everyone here for coming to this year's first annual Meira Winter Camp." Before he could say more, he was interrupted by a wave of cheering and applause.

"I also want to thank the kitchen staff, who have made us some fantastic meals this week," Glenn continued, setting off more applause. Everyone turned to the kitchen window, where Nadine, Corey, and her other foster children, all of whom had joined her for the day, waved and smiled.

"And most of all, I want to thank Scott, Genevieve, and Jeremy for Winter Camp color war. This was the most fun I've had outside in the snow—snow I didn't have to shovel, I might add—since I was a kid. I hope we can do it again next year."

The cheers grew louder, and Jeremy made his way to the front to stand with Scott, nodding his thanks to the families who called his name. Gen's happiness seemed to light up the room. As exhausted as they were, it had been worth it.

Then Glenn turned to Scott and said in a voice that held deeper notes of meaning, "Can we expect this much fun or more this coming summer?"

"More," Scott answered, the tense grin on his face melting into a genuine smile. "If you enjoyed winter camp, summer is even better— and warmer. With absolutely no snow, guaranteed."

"Unless we make some," Jeremy said. "With the ice maker. At night."

Gen covered her mouth to keep from laughing aloud, but he could tell from the way her eyes narrowed that she was wondering how it might be possible to make snow during the summer. He already had plans in his notebook that he'd show her later.

Glenn's voice interrupted his thoughts. "I hope I see all of you this coming summer. Scott, I know you'll be here. Genevieve, Jeremy, what about you?"

Gen smiled and nodded, setting off some shrieks from the girls who had been in her cabin the previous summer.

Jeremy had to clear his throat before he spoke, the words not fitting in his throat. "Not me, I'm afraid."

Gen spun around and looked at him.

"Gotta go be a grown-up. Summers off aren't so easy." He could see a few parents nodding, especially those who had been campers themselves and missed the freedom of summers at camp. "But I promise to visit—if I can borrow Scott's golf cart."

"Maybe," Scott said, while firmly shaking his head no.

Glenn said something else, but Jeremy didn't hear it. He was watching Genevieve. She looked pale, and angry, and miserable, like the light within had gone out.

He wasn't coming back for summer camp. This was really it. This was their last real time together at Meira.

It made sense, even though she didn't like it. She knew he was stressed, that he'd had to bargain with his brother to get the week off at all. He'd had to check his phone several times a day, hiking out to where there was a reliable signal every time. That wasn't really time off. That was like hitting pause.

Of course he couldn't come back next summer. His work, his real life, would intrude too much, even if he came for a few weeks. And visiting for the day would never be the same. A lot of former camp staff thought visiting for the day would let them recapture the experience of being at camp for the summer, but it never worked. A day never equaled a summer. Jeremy knew that as well as she did.

For a moment, she closed her eyes, admitting to herself in the privacy behind her own eyelids that she didn't think she'd enjoy camp nearly as much if he wasn't there. Second session last year hadn't been as much fun. A whole summer at Meira without him would be…an adjustment. Or a bigger word than that. Not just an adjustment for her. It would be incomplete.

Glenn thanked everyone once again, and Scott took over the attention of the room.

"If there's no more announcements, then I think it's time to award the first Meira Winter Camp color war crown—"

"Wait! I have one more thing." Gen opened her eyes and held up one hand. "Can I have three minutes?"

"Take four," Scott replied, gesturing at her to continue.

Gen jumped behind the woodpile and dragged a cardboard box out into the room. Jeremy moved to help her, but she stopped him with a shake of her head.

"Traditionally, we have camp shirts," she said, dusting her hands off on her ski pants. "And while it's not T-shirt weather right now, unless you're Jeremy—"

She glanced over at him and her mouth went dry. He was holding his notebook and her phone, standing against the wall of windows that looked out over the dying bonfire. His attention was on her, that intense focus that felt as if he was touching every part of her, all at once. She had to clear her throat before she could continue.

"Anyway, I hope you'll take these home to wear when it gets warmer, and maybe even bring them back next summer." Gen opened the box in front of her, the same one she'd pulled out of the storage pit. "A word to the laundry kings and queens in the room: these have not been set with a final wash. So keep them away from heat. Wash cold, turn them inside out and tumble dry low—or hang them on a line the first time, okay?"

She reached in and lifted the top shirt, holding it up by the shoulder seams so everyone could see it. It was a Camp Meira shirt, with the camp logo on the chest where a pocket would be if it had one. Gen had screen printed additional images onto the front, adding a menorah with candles to the pine tree and campfire of the Meira logo. Above the menorah it read, *We lit the flames...*

The Gen turned the shirt around so everyone could see the other side. A larger image of a campfire filled the back, and the words around the image read, *for next summer's bonfire! Meira Winter Camp 2014.*

"Nice. Limited edition, too." Jeremy had moved to stand next to her, and his proximity made her nervous. Which was ridiculous, she told herself.

"Handmade," Gen added, handing out shirts to the adults. Jeremy picked up the folded pile of children's sizes to help her distribute them. The parents were exclaiming about the lettering, which was done in old-fashioned swoops and curls, as if each word were made of ribbon. A few were asking Gen how she'd managed to make them all so quickly.

"Practice." She checked sizes and made sure each adult had a shirt that would fit them.

Scott took one from the stack in Jeremy's hands and held it in front of him.

"This is terrific."

"Thank you," Gen said, glancing at him.

"No, thank you. You and Jeremy—this was…this was really something else. I owe you one."

"One? Like an extra day off this summer?" Gen tried not to look at Jeremy after she spoke, but she couldn't resist.

Scott raised one brow while the corners of his lips quivered a bit. "Maybe. If you don't steal my golf cart."

"Steal a golf cart? Impossible!" Jeremy tried to look aghast, but his expression oversold the attempt. "I—*Gen* would *never* do such a thing."

Then Glenn tapped Genevieve's shoulder.

"Did you get a shirt, Glenn?"

"I did, but I wanted to ask you something. How do you calculate the winner? How much is each color war event worth?"

Gen's mouth opened, but she didn't know what to say. Color war event values were a closely guarded secret, shared only with the people who ran color war each summer. But Glenn was the boss.

Fortunately, Scott came to her rescue. "Sorry, Glenn. We can't tell. It's a camp secret. But if you come this summer, and help us run color war, we'll tell you everything."

Glenn's smile was immediate and very contagious. "I would really like that, and I'll make sure to clear my calendar when you have the dates."

"You should definitely judge some of the events," Jeremy said. "Oh! You can set up the scavenger hunt! I'll tell you all the good hiding places."

"There were things on that list that couldn't be found," Scott added. "Where did you hide everything? In the treetops?"

"Maybe."

Then Glenn turned to Jeremy, a serious expression on his face. "That reminds me. I know you're not able to come back next summer, Jeremy, which is a shame, but I do want to ask you a favor."

"Sure."

"How *do* you hot-wire a golf cart?"

Scott's mouth dropped open, and Genevieve squeezed her lips together to keep from laughing at his expression.

"I must know. Please. I would have so much fun this summer on the golf course."

"I will tell you all that you need to know—in a secret location to be named later," Jeremy said, shaking Glenn's hand.

"And you're invited for a round of golf, whenever you'd like."

Gen shook her head, pressing her smile into as flat an expression as possible. Jeremy invited for a round with the executive director. His dad would never believe it.

"Okay, now that everyone has their handmade, limited-edition Winter Camp shirt—thanks to Genevieve—it's time to announce the winning team." Scott held his arms up again to get everyone's attention, but it wasn't as effective. With the shirts plus the additional platters of cookies, brownies, and fruit that were being put out on the tables behind them, it took more than a few minutes for the room to be quiet enough for Gen and Jeremy to speak.

They needed those minutes, though, because when she pulled the notebook from Jeremy's hand, she saw that he hadn't finished tallying the score. Gen pulled him behind the woodpile so they could talk without being overheard.

"Jeremy, what were you doing?"

"I got distracted." His ears began to turn red. Gen huffed out an annoyed sigh.

"Give me my phone."

"Here's the score sheet. I think I added it right." He handed her a folded, very crumpled piece of notebook paper.

"You think I can add that column in my head? I need the calculator. Hand it over." She smacked him lightly on the chest with the back of her hand. He passed her phone over and looked at the screen as she unlocked it.

"You didn't even open the calculator, dude. Seriously. What were you doing?"

"Sorry—distracted. I told you." He pointed at the numbers on the lower right side of the paper. "I already added the columns earlier. That's the total as of this afternoon."

"So we add the plaque scores, which are here," Gen said, tapping on her phone. "And the cheer scores—which I'm assuming Scott gave you?"

Jeremy nodded, passing her a smaller sheet of paper, and Gen added the figures, then double-checked them.

"Guys? You ready? You need us to hang out here all night?" Scott had run out of stalling tactics.

Genevieve looked up at Jeremy.

"Ready?" His smile was contagious.

"Ready."

"Let's do this." As Gen slid her phone into her pocket, Jeremy lifted both arms and stepped out from behind the woodpile, hollering, "This is EPIC, PEOPLE!"

The campers responded as they always did, echoing his posture and yelling the word *epic* so loudly some of the parents covered their ears.

"No one will miss that," Gen said below the noise.

"Yeah, they will."

"You're right. I will." He froze, then looked at her. She didn't know if her expression communicated how she felt in that moment, a strange mix of excited and tired and sad that made her breath uneven. She was curious and more than a little turned on by the idea of staying with him in the staff cabin alone, but wary of the knowledge that this was probably the end of their time together at Meira. Her face must have shown some of what she felt, because he frowned. But then he gave her a look with such heat that she felt it like she felt his attention, so scorching she might need sunscreen.

She turned away and said to the crowd, "Who wants to know the winner?"

After calling for a tabletop drumroll and receiving some percussion assistance from Corey and his sisters, who tapped their cutting boards with pairs of wooden spoons, Gen held up her hands.

"The winner of the first—and I hope annual—Meira Winter Camp color war is: the white team!"

Mayhem erupted, with cheers and screaming and high fives under-scored by the good-natured though disappointed applause from the blue team. Gen hugged some of the campers from both teams and received handshakes and thanks from the parents. The noise subsided as the group slowly moved to gather around all the chocolate and fruit and eat as much of it as possible.

Jeremy sat down in front of a platter and built a stack of brownies, laughing as some of his former campers dared him to eat a world-record number of brownies. Gen made her way over to him, knowing he'd saved her a space at the table by his side.

"Well done, you two." Gen was climbing over the bench when Scott's voice made her look up.

"Thanks." Jeremy grinned around a large bite of chocolate.

"Jeremy, I know summer is impossible, but next winter, if we do this again and you want to come back, I will do everything I can to help you get time off," Scott said. "Even improve the cell service at camp."

"Oh, no, don't do that." Jeremy looked horrified. "That's one of the best parts of camp."

Scott laughed, then looked at Jeremy with an expression Gen hadn't seen before. "I mean that. You are always welcome and needed here, any time you can join us."

Jeremy swallowed and nodded, and Gen suspected he wasn't able to speak. She opened her mouth to say something, to cover the silence, but Scott interrupted. "One more thing, both of you."

He looked around to make sure no one was listening, and he sounded terribly serious. Gen put her hand on Jeremy's shoulder.

"I know you're both staying in the head staff cabin, by the fireplace. No, um…you know the rules."

Gen stared at Scott, mouth open in shock, a blush spreading across her face like fire on dry kindling. She didn't want to move her hand away from Jeremy, but she cursed herself for touching him in the first place.

"Dude," Jeremy said, voice low. "Not necessary."

"Yes, dude. Necessary." Scott lowered his chin to look at Jeremy, then at Gen. He was using his *you are in so much trouble* voice, perfected after many summers running a camp full of kids between the ages of seven and sixteen and staff between the ages of eighteen and horny. She would bet the red on her face extended over her scalp and probably down both arms.

Without another word, Scott moved away to talk to parents who were waiting for a moment with him.

"I cannot believe he just said that," Gen muttered as she climbed over the bench and took a seat.

"I can. It's his job."

"But—"

"Don't worry about it. It's cool. Or cold, even."

He smiled at her, but his cheeks above his beard were just as red. At least she wasn't alone in being embarrassed.

Jeremy pulled yet another brownie off the platter, then slid it closer so she could reach it. "We did it," he said.

"Yup."

"And was it?"

"Epic?"

"Yup."

"Yes, Jeremy, it was epic."

"You so didn't say that right."

Gen laughed and shook her head. "Embarrassing warnings aside, I think Scott seems a little more relaxed."

Jeremy nodded, then bent his head closer to her ear. Her heartbeat sped up, and she forced herself not to move away, or closer. "I heard him talking to Nadine earlier. Summer's on, and she's in, plus all her kids are hired, too."

Relief felt like the warmest summer day inside her.

"So, right now, everything's good." Jeremy took another bite of brownie and put his arm around her. She leaned into the solid warmth of his body and ate her cookie.

CHAPTER EIGHT

Saturday, December 20, 2014—29 Kislev 5775

They walked up to the cabin together, Jeremy following Gen this time, and when they got there, it was colder than she'd expected. Jeremy got to work building a mammoth fire, and then picked up the cot mattresses that were leaning against the couch.

"I have this all figured out." He laid the mattresses down end to end, the long side of each facing the fire. Gen got her sleeping bags and pillow from her room, which was indeed much colder than the living room, while Jeremy unrolled his. Then he spread a layer of blankets over each one, folding them at the bottom of each bed.

They brushed their teeth in a silence that wasn't oppressive but seemed dense with possibility and unspoken words. Then, mattresses tucked as close to the fire as safely possible, Jeremy and Gen zipped themselves into their sleeping bags, each one facing the hearth. The room was entirely lit by the blaze, and it was so bright Gen couldn't look directly at it. So she looked at Jeremy.

"I feel like I'm sleeping in a condom. I hate sleeping bags," Jeremy groused in a whisper.

"Well, they both protect you from…something. In this case, cold air and ass splinters."

"They still suck."

"Yes, they do."

They were quiet for a minute, the only sound Jeremy punching his pillow and Gen shifting her position, the nylon of her sleeping bag rubbing against the vinyl camp mattress with a long hissing sound.

"*And* we sound like snakes. I'm telling you. Sleeping bags are the worst."

"Well, we don't have many other options." Not options she could say out loud. After Scott's warning, she wasn't even sure there were options. They were adults, for crying out loud. But rules were rules, and she knew them as well as Jeremy did.

"Why are we whispering?" Jeremy asked aloud, his deep voice filling the room, reaching into the corners.

"Good question." She started to laugh. "We're the only ones here."

She turned onto her side and looked at him, and the unspoken tension turned into laughter that she couldn't stop.

Then a log collapsed in the fireplace, raising a burst of sparks, a few of which flew through the screen. They jumped up and slapped the sparks against the ground with their hands tucked into their sleeves. Once they were out, Jeremy swept the bits of ash back into the hearth, and they moved their mattresses and blankets away from the fire.

"Maybe this wasn't such a good idea," Jeremy muttered.

"I think we'll be okay." She wasn't entirely convinced, though.

"I'm moving us back a bit more." Even though it meant she'd probably be colder than she wanted to be, she had to agree with him.

With their mattresses farther away from the fireplace, they climbed back into their respective sleeping bags, head to head, still facing the warmth. Their mattresses overlapped slightly, though, and when Genevieve pulled her sleeping bag over her shoulders and slid her arms across her pillow, she hit Jeremy on the head. That seemed as good a signal as any that things were not happening that night.

"Sorry."

"No worries. You can hit on me anytime."

"You're a prince among men, Jeremy."

"I know."

He pulled his long-sleeved shirt off, revealing a worn camp T-shirt beneath. She looked away and closed her eyes. It was time to go to sleep and stop thinking about alternative ways to warm up in the cold.

"Good night, Jer." Gen leaned forward to kiss his cheek just as he turned his head. And then she was kissing him, almost on the mouth. It was like they'd bumped into each other, only with half their lips instead of arms or shoulders, a completely motionless almost kiss, awkward and terrible, each waiting a beat for the other to move, neither willing to be first.

And then it changed.

Jeremy reached across her pillow and touched her face, curving his fingers around the back of her head, weaving gently through her hair to hold her still.

"Please don't move." His lips were a breath apart from hers.

"Wasn't planning on it."

When he kissed her again, she breathed in the scent of him, a smell of the cloves from the spice box and wood smoke from the bonfire mixing with the hot temptation of his mouth. There wasn't any wine in her bloodstream, but the heat she'd felt every time they kissed raced through her again, knocking aside any flimsy boundaries that might have remained between them.

"Gen?" His voice was a whisper again.

"Yeah?"

"I…would you…come over here? Join me in my nonspliffy sleeping bag?"

She smiled at him and moved her hand to unzip her own when he reached out to stop her movement.

"I want you. You know that, right?" She frowned, but nodded. He looked nervous.

"Okay, good. Because we are not having sex tonight."

She gaped at him.

"I mean, I don't know if you thought…and I didn't want to hurt you or make you feel unwanted but—no. I can't."

"You *can't?*" This was more awkward than bump-kissing him. Gen didn't know what to say. *Please visit my sleeping bag but I'm not sleeping with you* was not what she'd expected, and she had no idea how to respond.

He shook his head, his eyes focused on her, so intent she couldn't move or look away.

"You don't get it. I have been dreaming of…you, thinking about this for so long, and there is no way we're doing it on the floor in subzero weather in too-small sleeping bags."

"Okay." She spoke slowly, elongating the word, still very confused.

Jeremy moved his hand so that it covered her fingers, which were gripping the edge of her pillow.

"I told you last night, you have no idea—"

"So why are you saying no?"

"I'm not saying not ever." He laughed, but it sounded more like nervousness than humor. "I'd never say that. But I am saying not here. Not when we're cold and I worry we might fall through the floor."

"You seriously think we'd fall through the floor?"

He shrugged.

"But…another time?" Gen was still baffled by the boundaries he was setting.

"I hope so."

"But you're not coming back next summer."

He looked at her strangely. "We do exist outside of camp, Gen."

She blinked. "We do? I mean, I know we do but…"

"Wait, did you think this was like a camp hookup for me?" Now he looked angry, his eyebrows down, his cheeks turning red.

"No, not at all. But…oh, hang on a minute. Stay there." With cold fingers, she yanked open the zipper on her sleeping bag and crawled toward Jeremy. He opened the side of his bag and welcomed her by folding her into his arms, then covering her with the fabric and zipping it partway up behind her.

She was surrounded, warm and...hot, actually. But she wanted to finish what she'd been saying before she kissed him again.

"You were saying?" He was looking at the fire behind her. She reached up and tugged on his beard gently to get his attention.

"Hey! Mind the man beard."

"That's a man beard? There are different types? Like, what, a lumberjack beard?"

"Ooh, lumberjack beard. I should grow one. My dad would flip."

Gen smiled, but then propped her head on one hand to look at him. "I never thought I was a hookup for you."

"Good." Jeremy moved his head back a little.

"But I also thought you might be coming back next summer."

"There's no way. You saw how many messages I had. A whole summer? There's no way."

"So this really is it." She spoke more to herself than to him, but he heard her.

He looked down, a frown on his face. "No, it's not. I don't understand why you think that. Do you disappear when you leave camp? Shoveled sidewalks and consistent heat and the magic of food delivery cause you to dissolve?"

"No, but...Jeremy. We never see each other at home."

"I was at school. Then you were in Iceland. We're both home now."

"Yes, that's true, but..." She blew out a breath, looked down, and then focused on him again. "Okay, what are you doing tomorrow?"

"Going home."

"After that?"

"Going to work?"

"Exactly. I don't know when I'd see you."

"We can work this out very easily. I work weird hours, yes, but I do not work all the time. I can—get this—drive a car to come see you. I can even bring pizza."

Gen lowered her head to his pillow and looked up at him while he spoke. Her arms were tucked against his chest, and she allowed herself to slowly explore the hard curves of his shoulders, the strength of his arms.

"Stop that. I can't think if you do that." He pulled her tighter against him so she couldn't move her arms so easily. "Genevieve, it's never going to be as easy as it is here, but…it's not impossible."

"Okay," she said, nodding. She knew, though she didn't say so, that it wouldn't be as simple as he said, that real life was going to get in the way. But at that moment, it was simple. He was right there, and she wanted to explore him. And they could figure out what happened next some other time.

"Are you sure?"

She nodded again. "Can I please move my hands now?"

"Are you going back to your bag?"

"In a minute," she said with a smile.

"Okay," he said, his own smile matching hers until he leaned closer and kissed her.

Everywhere he put his hands, she felt warm. His lips moved over hers with so much variety of contact, she wanted to start making a list of the different types of kisses. But she was distracted by his touch before she could catalog more than two.

He slid his palm down the curve of her hip, and she wondered if her skin glowed in the wake of his touch, an incandescent acknowledgment of her wanting more. She could be a night-light, she thought. The more he touched her the greater the illumination.

Every part of her skin felt like she'd come inside from being out too long in the cold. His touch was like heat, so welcome, and so painful, like plunging frozen hands into warm water. Despite the tingling burn, she couldn't pull away.

The way he made her feel, hot and liquid like burning oil, she didn't want any more boundaries between them. She grabbed his arms with both hands and held on before she moved her hands beneath the edge of his shirt, feeling his shiver when her fingertips moved over his skin. She knew what his chest looked like. If she added up the hours she'd spent with him when he didn't have a shirt on, that time might be measured in years. But knowing what he looked like was nothing compared to learning how he felt, and how he reacted.

She moved her fingers through the hair covering his abdomen, feeling the ridges of his muscles contract with her touch. The more she touched him, the deeper he kissed her, until touch and taste had mingled into a single overwhelming sensation.

They kissed for what might have been hours, or might have been ten minutes. Gen had no idea. There was no way to tell time when her world reached no farther than his lips, his tongue, his hands on her back, her hips, and the curving path she traced across the flexing muscles of his arms and his back. She wanted more light so she could see her fingertips exploring the terrain of his body. She wanted to follow her hands with her eyes and her mouth, learn the taste and texture of every part of him.

She lay facing him and found she could only map his skin the way she wished with one hand. The other was pinned beneath her. Jeremy could reach her with one hand as well, and they broke apart at the same moment to shift position, to try to move toward one another. His smile, so close to her, made her want more of him, and she grinned as she freed her arm and tried to push him onto his back.

"Oh, no," he said, pretending to fight back yet allowing her to slide over him.

But then the fabric of the sleeping bag, already pulled tight beneath his body, trapped her, and she couldn't move toward him at all. He tried to lift his back and move the fabric beneath him to give her more room, but it didn't work and only made the constriction worse. She started to laugh.

"Gen, I hate sleeping bags like you have no idea right now." He wrapped one arm around her as he rolled to the side to try to fix their very small, very limited space.

Then she heard boots crunching in the snow below the windows, heading toward the cabin door.

"Shit," Jeremy breathed.

Gen slid out of the sleeping bag as fast as she could and dove back into her own, wrapping the open side around her and dropping her head to her pillow. Those footsteps turned into stomping as someone, probably Scott, cleared the snow from their boots. Then the door opened.

"Hey, kids," Scott said, an awkward smile on his face. Jeremy looked at him, and Gen wasn't sure she could trust herself not to start babbling with nervousness, so she waved.

"You guys okay up here?"

"Yup," Jeremy said. "Plenty of wood standing by."

Gen pressed her face down into the pillow and bit the corner to keep from laughing aloud. She was going to kill Jeremy. Twice.

"Right," Scott said. "It shouldn't be as cold as it was last night, but if it starts to get dangerous or unsafe up here, I want you two to move to some of the family cabins, got it?"

Jeremy nodded. "Understood."

Gen rolled to her side and bit the inside of her cheek as she looked up and nodded at Scott.

"I'll stop letting the cold air in now," Scott said finally, backing out of the cabin and shutting the door. "Good night."

Gen waited until the crunch of Scott's boots in the snow receded into the distance before she looked at Jeremy.

"Dude. Seriously?"

He smirked at her.

"*Plenty of wood standing by?* Oh, my God, Jeremy. I think my mouth is bleeding from biting my tongue."

"He left, didn't he?"

"You might as well have waved a flag made of condoms at him."

"That's not a bad idea for next summer." Then his face changed, and he looked at her, a little sadly. "Think you could pull that off?"

"There is nothing I want to do that includes condoms if you're not involved."

Jeremy snorted. Then he unzipped his bag.

"Where are you going? Are you leaving?"

"Nope." He stood and pulled his mattress away from her. She felt cold slice through her chest. He was moving away.

Then he spun his bed around and slid it alongside hers, placing her between himself and the fire, then dropped his pillow behind hers. He climbed back into his sleeping bag, zipped it up, and moved closer to her.

Gen rolled over onto her back. The fire covered his face with moving light and shadows and she watched him as he gazed at her.

"Scott's such a mood killer." She was whispering again, though she had no reason to.

"Yeah. Come closer? Please?"

She slid across her mattress with the hiss of nylon against nylon, and he moved one arm beneath her to bring her closer. His eyes were a thousand shades of green and gold, and she wasn't sure she'd be able to sleep. Maybe she should count them instead of sheep. He'd have to stay awake. She could keep him awake.

"I'm sorry," he whispered, his lips moving against hers when he spoke. She nodded.

She understood his apology. And he was right. As much as she wanted to rip off their clothes and run for the finish line, it didn't seem quite right. They needed to find space for one another when they weren't at Meira, to figure out how to keep going when they weren't in the suspended reality of camp.

"Did you set an alarm?" She nodded again. "Six?"

"No, five thirty, unfortunately."

"Ugh. Why so early?"

"The bus might arrive any time after six. So I have to be up at the gate."

"I'll go with you." The tip of his nose rubbed against hers.

"No, you have to go help load the luggage, I think. That's what it says on your schedule."

"Don't leave tomorrow without finding me."

"Wouldn't dream of it," she said, lifting her face to kiss him.

There wasn't blazing intensity like there had been moments before. His kiss was slow, and gentle, like falling into bed, warm and safe, more comfort than possibility.

"Good night," he whispered.

"Night," she replied. Then she rolled over, facing the fire, and heard him move closer behind her. She could feel the solid warmth of his body through her sleeping bag and his, and his arm was still curved beneath her. She slid lower on her pillow until his arm was beneath her neck so his hand wouldn't go numb. Then she slid her fingers slowly between his, watching the light flicker over their hands before she fell asleep.

Sunday, December 21, 2014—29 Kislev 5775

When she woke up, Jeremy was already gone. He'd tucked his blankets over her, and she'd slept until her alarm went off. His sleeping bag was cold. He'd left wood burning in the fireplace, but the log was more gray than black, so it had been burning awhile.

The morning was a blur of cold wind and an evolving to-do list. To her relief, the gate motor was working, so she opened it easily for the bus, which arrived at precisely 6:02, just as she'd expected. After a split-second breakfast, she said good-bye to the Winter Camp families, promising them a special private gallery of the pictures she'd taken when she was got home. Once they were all loaded onto the bus headed back to the city, the camp grew silent, but her day increased in speed.

Scott, Jeremy, Genevieve, and the kitchen staff all had tasks to complete to close up camp after the families left, but each item Genevieve checked off spawned three more. She bundled up the laundry from each bunk, but then had to find a working vehicle to bring it to the office. Once all the blankets, spare towels, and extra cot sheets were at the office, she had to find a laundry bag, since all of the summer bags were packed up somewhere, and she didn't have time to look. By the time lunch was ready, she was exhausted and so cold she felt brittle. She still had things to do, but they were, mercifully, all tasks that she could complete inside. Preferably near a fire, if not sitting in the hearth itself.

She wrapped her fingers around her paper cup of tea, wondering if she should get one for each hand. Scott sat down in front of her, pulling off his cap and shaking ice from his hair.

"Whoa. Where were you?"

"Checking the platforms, following all footprints to make sure no supplies were left outside."

"Oh, no, I'm sorry. A lot of those were mine or Jeremy's. We could have told you that those areas were clear as of last night."

Scott shook his head. "I still have to check them myself."

Genevieve nodded, then looked around. "Where is Jeremy?"

"On the turnpike by now, I think."

Gen stared at him.

"He didn't find you before he left?"

She shook her head slowly, trying to breathe through a disappointment that burned her throat.

"His dad called this morning—called the camp office." Scott's eyebrows disappeared into his hairline. "He was lucky I was there. Said he needed Jeremy to get back as soon as possible."

"Did something happen?"

Scott shrugged. "No idea. Just asked me to tell Jeremy to check his phone and then get home ASAP. Jeremy said he was going to find you before he left."

"I was all over the place this morning. I would have been hard to find." She spoke mostly to herself.

Last year, he hadn't told her why he was leaving, but he'd said goodbye. Now, she knew why he'd had to go, but he hadn't found her, hadn't spoken to her before he left. Either way, it hurt.

They finished eating but didn't hang around the dining hall despite the warmth and the very peaceful silence. Nadine and her kids were leaving after lunch and needed to wash the dishes they'd used. Plus, she still needed to pack.

Walking into the cabin with Scott made her face grew hot, matching the burn deep in her chest. Jeremy had moved the mattresses back and placed her pillow on the bed in her room. Her camp sleeping bag was rolled up into a perfect coil, and the blankets they'd used were folded and stacked on a shelf. He'd cleaned up every sign that they'd spent the night on the floor snuggled together, kissing until they were interrupted.

The silence of the cabin hurt her ears and pressed on her skin. Scott was whistling through his teeth as he threw the last of his own things in a bag, unaffected by the space that Gen found so disorienting. Her clothes were easy to pack, and Jeremy had bundled everything else for her. But his room was empty, the bed and the shelves bare, the door between their rooms propped open like no one had been there at all. The absence of his stuff everywhere, sprawled across every surface like Jeremy sprawled on the couch, was almost as loud as his presence, the quiet hurting her ears.

So she hurried, throwing her things haphazardly in her duffel, since it didn't matter much. Everything had to be washed anyway. She just wanted to leave. She was about to ask Scott a question when his walkie-talkie buzzed three times.

"Someone's at the gate," he said, pulling his hat back on.

"I'm done packing, so I'll get it. Stay and finish so we can get home before dark." She pulled on her gloves. "Can I borrow your keys?"

Scott tossed them to her. "Better than you hot-wiring my truck."

"I only know how to hot-wire golf carts."

She pushed the door open with her back, her duffel over her shoulder and the sleeping bag under her arm. She'd bring it home to wash, then return it next summer during staff week.

As she drove slowly up the hill, she had to turn down the radio that Scott had left somewhere up near eardrum-blast level. She knew now what song he'd been whistling, and the whistling was preferable.

A dark red truck waited at the gate, and the driver waved at Gen as she pulled over and jumped down to the ground. She'd pressed the button to open the gates, but instead of stepping to the side of the road, she walked through them as they swung open. The driver rolled down his window when she approached.

"I was hoping I'd see you today," she said with a grin, her heart beating faster. "How've you been?"

Two hours later, she was home. Every time she made the drive home from camp, she felt like it should take longer than it did. Once Scott's truck was off the two-lane blacktop road and on the highway, though, within minutes the blur of trees and mountains dropped away, and the blur of buildings, gas stations, and houses took over. Most of them showed off holiday lights in a multitude of colors, giving her a reason to keep her face turned away from Scott. He didn't say very much, anyway, just that he was as tired as she was, and that her sleeping bag, no longer soaked but not clean either, was with the rest of the camp laundry. When Nadine picked it up next week, she'd leave it in the office for Gen to get next summer. One less thing for her to pack, he joked.

Scott dropped her off at her new apartment, thanking her one last time for staging a coup and changing the schedule—something he hadn't fully appreciated, but recognized had been a great success for him, and for Meira.

"I'll be calling you soon about next summer. You're still coming back, right?"

She looked at him in surprise. "I wouldn't miss it."

The silence of her apartment wasn't as painful as the silence at camp, but she was surprised how everything seemed slightly unfamiliar, despite the fact that she'd lived there for almost three months.

Gen dropped her things in the doorway and looked at her home. Her computer was there, her TV, her couch that she'd bought on sale, the pillows she'd made for it still perched in each corner. She knew everything was hers, but it was all so new that, after a week in a place she knew by heart, being home felt odd.

Kicking her duffel into the kitchen where the washer and dryer hid in a closet, she pulled off a few of the layers she'd lived in for the past week and tossed those on top of her bag. One sleeve hit the front of the fridge and knocked down one of the magnets holding up a picture. The front of her refrigerator was covered with printouts of the photos she'd shared online from Iceland, with the captions Jeremy had added.

She picked up the image that had fallen down to pin it back on the door, a shot she'd taken from Mount Esja last December, when the sun rose well after eleven in the morning. She'd captioned that one before Jeremy could: *Now THAT is a late wake-up.*

When she sat down to eat dinner, the sky outside her window was shifting from faded peach to dark blue. She'd placed the table that also served as her desk against the wall under the picture window so she could see the sun or the stars while she ate or worked. An image of the night sky over Iceland now leaned against the napkin holder in front of her, the entire frame filled with the glowing plume of the Milky Way.

At camp, there was a limitless sky with a never-ending sweep of stars above their limited world. Some of those same stars were appearing now, the brightest ones that could shine past the lights of the city. She was still under the same sky, the same winter stars, even if they couldn't all be seen.

When the dryer beeped at her, she pulled the elastic straps off the sleeping bag she'd used and unrolled it so she could unzip the fabric into a large square. It looked so strange on her living room carpet, like something from another planet. She reached across to pull the zipper and heard a crunching noise inside. Leaves or twigs, or so she thought, but when she reached inside, she found notebook paper.

Jeremy's notebook paper, the paper they'd used to schedule color war events, and come up with competitions and plan the last five days.

But there wasn't a schedule on this page. In a scrawling diagonal across the lines, Jeremy had written,

Genevieve—

I have to leave early. Doody calls. Or my dad does. Anyway. I'll call you.

This week has been one of the best of my life. It was epic.

I'll miss you.

—J

Then, at the bottom, in smaller letters, he'd added, *I miss you already.*

Gen sat with the paper in her hand, reading it over and over, before placing it on the table next to her laptop, which she'd just turned on for the first time in a week. Her in-box flooded with new messages, the computer beeping as each one arrived. They were easy to sort, but as she scanned the list a second time, she noticed there wasn't one from Jeremy.

His note leaned against the napkin holder, next to her photo of the sky, and she looked at the photo, his caption cut off by the printer, one that had made her laugh every time she looked at it. Had there been meaning behind the captions, something more behind the jokes he made? Probably, but she still had no idea what to say to him now that she was home. She could talk to him about anything at camp, even start a conversation in the middle of a sentence, and he'd understand immediately. Now that she was home, and so was he, she didn't know how or where to begin.

Genevieve set up her work for the following morning and sketched out her to-do list on a scrap of paper while the pictures from Winter Camp copied from the camera's memory card. Somehow, she'd taken nearly four hundred pictures in five days.

Those were less easy to sort. She was able to delete blurry images and pictures that caught people in awkward moments or only half in the frame, but there were more than 250 left when she was done.

So many of Jeremy, too. Leading cheers. Rolling a giant snowball to help the white team build a snowman in his likeness, even though he technically wasn't supposed to assist them. Challenging campers in sled races down the hill, throwing snowballs, trying to play baseball in waist-high snowdrifts using plastic bats, every image featuring red noses and huge smiles.

The she found a picture toward the end that she didn't recognize. She hadn't taken it. She couldn't have.

She was in it.

She was standing with Ella by the bonfire, helping her make a s'more while keeping the melted marshmallow from getting all over the little girl's mittens. She was laughing and licking her fingers, but behind her, Jeremy was watching her.

His hands were in his pockets as he stood. Glenn was talking to him, gesturing with one hand, but while Jeremy might have been listening, his attention was focused on Genevieve.

The bonfire lit his face so she could see his expression clearly. He was half smiling, his eyes gentle and his expression proud and almost wondrous. And he was looking at her.

Seeing his emotions so plain on his face filled her with the same warmth she'd felt in his arms the night before and hiking by his side for the past few days. Gen thought about all the ways he'd cared for her over the past week, and all the things he'd done that she'd only just learned about. He'd been beside her for some of the best moments of her life, and he'd been behind her for some of the worst, doing everything he could to help her. He'd seemed so confident that their relationship could continue outside of camp, that things would be the same the next time they saw each other. She wasn't sure if that was true, but she knew she missed him more now than she had at the end of every summer they'd spent together.

Genevieve stayed up for another hour, sorting pictures and loading them onto the camp website in a special gallery for the Winter Camp families. The one of her by the fire with Ella stayed open on her desktop, and after looking at it repeatedly, she set it as the wallpaper on her computer. When she shut down her laptop, all the programs disappeared one by one, until all that remained was the image, with the edge of the fire illuminating her laughter as she licked marshmallow from her fingers, and Jeremy standing behind, watching over her. When the screen went dark, she added one more thing to her to-do list for the following day.

She didn't wash the sleeping bag that night. She put it on her bed—

after she checked it for leaves and rocks or, worse, anything creepy or crawly—and used it as a blanket. It didn't really need to be washed, not right away.

Jeremy sat down on his bed, holding his phone. He had no new voice mail messages, no new e-mail, not a single indicator that anyone wanted to talk to him. It was confusing.

That morning, the farther he'd driven from camp, the more his phone had beeped as a flood of messages arrived. The stupid thing had almost sounded relieved, like the cellular company was finally able to unload all the crap it had saved for him.

All day, his phone had worked perfectly. He didn't have to go anywhere; anyone who needed to reach him found him. His phone had vibrated in his pocket so often, he'd thought at first something was wrong with it. But no, it was working, signaling that there was yet another problem, yet another matter to be addressed, with two funerals on the schedule for the next day, then two more the day after that.

Jeremy changed his clothes, hanging his black suit next to his five other black suits and his three gray ones, and pulled on clean sweatpants. His wardrobe at home consisted of two classes of clothing: apparel that could theoretically be destroyed at camp and suits for the most somber of occasions, with nothing in between.

He answered a text from his dad and updated the funeral schedule on the website from his phone before looking in his in-box again. Mixed in among a few legitimately important messages were things he easily deleted, but he looked through his trash again to make sure he hadn't deleted something from Genevieve.

No messages. Nothing from her e-mail, no texts, and nothing online, either. He wasn't sure what time Scott had finally left, but she had to be home by now. At camp, there were just two ways to talk to people: in person, or over the walkie-talkies. Now that they were home, there were sixty zillion ways to talk to someone, and he couldn't figure out which one to use, or if he should, or what he should say.

Jeremy shook his head at himself while he fixed himself dinner. His debate over how to to contact Gen, and what to say, was making him tense, and angry at himself. But he couldn't tell himself honestly that it wasn't that big of a deal.

It was a big deal. For him, anyway. The night before, he'd been next to Genevieve, her head resting on his arm, her fingers wound around his. Technically, they'd slept together before, in the literal sense. But after she'd fallen asleep, he'd been kept awake, not by his arm going numb under her head, but by the memory of another night in adjacent sleeping bags the year before.

They'd been on a campout, the two of them and some of the junior OA staff, plus a group of campers whose ability to maintain their cabin in absurd levels of neatness had earned them a special trip before the end of the first session. They'd gone canoeing, then hiking through some waterfalls before setting up camp and eating a dinner that included so much food, the OA staff still called it the Great Feast. Nadine had outdone herself.

With full stomachs and a day of paddling and hiking behind them, everyone had fallen asleep almost instantly. Jeremy had volunteered to stay up and tend the fire until it was safe for him to go sleep. When he'd climbed into his sleeping bag next to Gen's, only her curls had been visible. She'd pulled her sleeping bag over her head so only the tips of her hair showed in the firelight.

Unable to stop himself, he'd leaned close to her and reached over to touch her hair, and she'd pushed the edge of her sleeping bag away from her face. He'd thought he was busted, that she was going to ask him what he was doing and he'd have to come up with some reason for his behavior other than, "Your hair is beautiful and I really wanted to touch it."

But she'd been asleep. He'd remained still, making sure she stayed that way, when she lifted her head slightly and moved toward him. She'd found the space beneath his outstretched arm, next to his chest, and snuggled against him, her hair spreading out behind her on the pillow. Once he realized she wasn't waking up or moving away, he'd rolled onto his side facing her, and eventually fallen asleep that way.

He'd woken up in nearly the same position, with her head still nestled against his chest, her hair across his arm, and his hand resting on her side. He'd been the first one to wake up, so no one else saw him open his eyes and hold his breath.

He knew, in that moment, he wanted to wake up like that for the rest of his life. He wanted to wake up with Gen beside him—maybe not on the ground outside, but with her next to him at the start of every day.

The leaves above him had formed a canopy in silhouette against the golden light of the sunrise, and his eyes had stared at the outlines while his mind had moved at the speed of sound. She was about to study abroad through a fellowship for over a year, and her graduate studies were going to take up the next few years of her life after that. But she knew where she was going, what she was doing next. He had to get his crap together, figure out his life outside of camp if he wanted her to be part of it. He'd applied to a mortuary program, but wasn't able to begin coursework until the fall. His plan had been to only take on a part-time schedule.

That morning, he'd known that he needed to take charge of his own life and make real decisions, not half-assed plans. He needed to identify what he was going to do, what came next for him, so he'd be ready for what he was pretty sure would be the last relationship he'd have.

He wanted Genevieve in his life, and he knew that if he had the chance to be with her, not just at camp but everywhere, that would be it for him. She was it for him. When the message from his father arrived that a space in the mortuary sciences summer program had opened up for him, he'd taken it as a sign and talked to Scott immediately about leaving camp early.

His one regret was that he'd chickened out before telling Gen the reason he was leaving and that he'd decided what his career would be, that after so much time feeling unsure, his decisions had felt entirely right. He hadn't been able to explain any of it easily, so he hadn't tried. But talking to Gen in the woods during Winter Camp had been almost easy, as if he'd been ready to tell her everything.

Well, almost everything. He still wasn't sure how to say, "Listen, we never talked about this, but I'm in love with you and…yeah."

Sitting down with his dinner and the mail that had piled up in his absence, Jeremy flipped through the photographs on his phone until he found the one he'd taken just after the snow-sculpture building and the scavenger hunt had begun. He'd taken it by accident, trying to capture the whole field in one frame. But instead of zooming out, he'd zoomed in and taken a picture without meaning to, capturing Genevieve as she'd started to laugh. When he'd seen the image, he'd had that same feeling in his chest as he'd had that morning on the campout last year, like his body was collapsing and expanding at the same moment. She was still it for him.

He finished eating, sorted the mail, and checked his phone. Still nothing new, no one looking for him, no new messages.

He got into bed a short while later, his exhaustion finally catching up to him. He was alone in a very warm room, with very warm sheets on a very warm bed—one that was entirely silent, too. There were no bedsprings squealing in outrage every time he breathed, no mattress rubbing against his sleeping bag sounding like two nylon windbreakers getting frisky.

He liked the warmth and the quiet, but he missed camp. He missed the sound of the trees, the way his clothes always smelled like wood smoke, the hush that indicated more snow had covered the ground. Each morning, he'd woken up stunned that their tracks and the paths they'd shoveled had been partially or entirely filled in with more white, like a blank slate greeting him with each muted sunrise.

There wasn't any snow in the forecast that he knew of, but tomorrow could be a blank slate, too.

CHAPTER NINE

Tuesday, December 23, 2014—2 Tevet 5775
Eighth night of Hanukkah

The sidewalk beneath Genevieve's boots was clear of snow and ice. Tiny pellets of salt crunched beneath her as she walked. She didn't have to raise her knees to step over yet another waist-high drift of hardened snow. The path in front of her was made of precise, almost perfect slices cut through the snow on either side of the concrete.

She still watched her step. Despite the shoveled sidewalk and salted pavement, she expected branches and rocks beneath the snow. She wasn't walking quickly, either, and she knew it wasn't because of imagined roots on the path. Gen looked down at the box in her arms and tried to stop herself from checking again and again to make sure the light was on in Jeremy's apartment.

He lived in a complex that looked like many others around it, square and built in blocks around courtyards with perfectly trimmed hedges now topped with flat shelves of snow. All the apartments were lit with holiday lights except one—the windows she was pretty sure were his. Jeremy was the northeast corner of no Christmas.

She climbed the few stairs and with her knuckle pressed the button next to the name tag that read J-Goldy. His name tag at camp had sometimes read "J-Go," "Jewy Goldness," and for a brief moment before Scott made him change it, "J-G-d." "J-Goldy" was tame in comparison, but it still made her smile behind her scarf.

When she pressed the buzzer again, though, the door didn't open. She didn't hear the lock disengage, and she looked around for a different doorbell. Maybe she'd pressed the wrong one. Or maybe he wasn't home, she thought, closing her eyes.

She'd finally texted him that morning, after sleeping fitfully, waking up every few hours anxious and disoriented. She hadn't bothered to get out of bed before she grabbed her phone to text him. When she pulled up their message history, though, she'd noticed the picture was different.

She opened his contact information. He'd altered it.

Where it said *Company* he'd typed, "Yours, please. Any time."

Under *Title*, he'd typed in all caps, "*EPIC!*"

He'd put in his new address, and under *Country* he'd written, "Please visit. No passport required. I promise it's warm here."

The picture was the part that surprised her most. She'd been using an old snapshot from when they were kids, of Jeremy at age ten with big teeth and skinny arms and legs.

But he'd taken another in the dining hall on the final night of Winter Camp. He was looking into the camera, wearing that smile that belonged to her. It was the way he looked at her when he was proud of her, when they'd pulled off something tremendous, or when she made him laugh too hard and he'd finally gotten control of himself.

Well, he had said he'd been too distracted to add up the color war scores. He'd been busy.

He'd replied to her message that, "DUDE YES," she should come over that night, and that he'd be home after six. It was nearly seven now.

Maybe he'd gotten stuck at work.

Then his voice came from the speaker near the doorbells.

"Hello?"

"Hi, Jeremy. It's me. Can you come down?"

"You don't want to come up? I can buzz you in."

"No, I...I need you to come down."

"On my way," he replied. His voice sounded distorted, like he'd moved too close to the microphone. A few moments later, she heard a door close, and then he appeared, jogging down the stairs.

She nearly fell over. He was wearing a suit. An actual suit, dark gray with pinstripes, and a tie. And cuff links. He had gold cuff links. She knew she was staring, but she couldn't help herself. Jeremy in a suit was…well, it was epic.

"Greetings, Genevieve." Was his voice saying her name always going to make her feel like fireflies had collected in the middle of her chest?

"Evening, sir. Package delivery."

"Dude. That box is huge. What is that?"

"Well, in the traditional way of our people, and of most people, I think, you open it to find out what's inside."

Lifting the carton between them, they maneuvered it up the stairs and around the corner into his apartment. It wasn't heavy, but it was awkward and unevenly weighted, and Gen couldn't manage it up a flight of stairs alone, though she felt guilty about possibly dirtying his suit.

She'd backed into his apartment, and after they put the carton down, Jeremy moved to stand in front of her.

"Hey," he said softly, pushing a piece of her hair away from her face. She wasn't sure what to do next, whether she should kiss him or ask about his day. His suit was disorienting her, and she didn't know what to say.

Then she turned, saw his apartment, and forgot everything else.

When she pictured Jeremy, it was usually in old T-shirts and soft, worn clothing, slouched on a couch at camp. But his home had real furniture that coordinated with the rug, and lamps that all matched one another. It was unexpectedly adult. It matched the Jeremy in front of her, wearing a suit.

Or part of a suit. He'd removed his jacket.

But then Gen noticed the walls. Pictures of Meira—of the trees, the lake, the empty lifeguard chairs, the horses in the stable, even a sepia-toned picture of the bunk beds in one of the tents—covered every surface. It looked like camp was peeking into the room through a patchwork of windows.

"Did you take these?"

"A few. You took some of them."

"I did? When?"

"For the camp yearbook, mostly." She felt Jeremy's hands on her shoulders and she turned her head to look up at him.

"Can I take your coat, my lady?"

She still wore what she considered camp clothes, worn hiking pants and four shirts in varying layers of thickness. With Jeremy wearing a tie, a loosened tie but a tie nonetheless, she felt weirdly underdressed. And really warm. She took off one shirt, then another. But when she pulled the second one over her head, she caught Jeremy staring before he turned away, looking down at the carton by the front door.

"So, can I ask what's in this giant-ass box you wouldn't let me carry?"

When she moved closer, she saw him glance at her lips, then her cheeks, his gaze running over her face before returning to her eyes.

She opened her mouth to say yes, he could open the box, but instead, she said, "I miss you."

"I know."

"No, I mean, since I last saw you. I miss you."

"I know. Me, too."

Then he smiled. "Please, can I open the box?"

"After we light candles?"

He frowned.

"It's the last night of Hanukkah."

"If you insist. Have you eaten?"

She shook her head.

"Perfect. I'm ordering pizza. It won't be Nadine's, but I'll live." He spun toward the kitchen, rubbing his hand over the top of his head, ruffling his hair into familiar disarray. "I think I have some wine, too. Want some?"

"Can I stay?"

He froze. "Of course. But we don't have to have wine if you don't want. I know you don't like to drive after…"

"No, I mean, even without wine." She swallowed, then took a breath. "I brought a bag. Thought if you weren't getting up too early, maybe I could stay."

He moved closer to her, sliding his hands around her waist. He'd unbuttoned the collar of his shirt, and beneath it, she could see an old, faded red Camp Meira T-shirt, one he'd worn every summer that she could remember. She reached up and touched the collar, soft and ragged.

"Even if I had to get up in an hour, which I don't, I would still want you to stay. I always want you to stay."

"Okay," she said softly.

But he didn't kiss her. He stepped back slowly and nodded toward the kitchen wall. "If you order the food, I'll go change."

She opened her mouth to tell him to wait, that she wanted to unbutton him, unwrap him to see if more of camp hid beneath the suited exterior, but if she stayed the night, she'd have another chance. Maybe she'd stay with him a few days. She had her laptop. She could work anywhere, and classes didn't start until January.

She placed the order, and a few moments later, Jeremy came down the hall wearing flannel pants and the old shirt that had been hidden beneath his suit. He looked like himself, and she still wanted to unwrap him.

"How long for delivery?" he asked, getting two wineglasses down from a cabinet.

"Thirty minutes."

"That long? I have to wait that long to open this giant box?" Jeremy looked horrified.

She took the glasses from his hands and pushed him toward the door.

"Fine, since you have no self-control. You can open it."

"I have excellent self-control." The scorching look he gave her over his shoulder made her mouth drop open.

Then he sighed with great windy drama and sat down in front of the carton. Inside were about sixteen million Styrofoam peanuts.

"Dude. You suck."

Gen laughed and gestured for him to dig in.

He pawed through the pile of peanuts, which interfered by sticking to his arms and his hair as the static electricity spread. "Seriously, Gen. You're evil."

"Keep digging," she said, standing behind him. He kept shoving piles of peanuts to one side, then the other, and finding nothing but more peanuts.

"What did you do, put a needle in here?"

"Keep going, you big whiner."

Then his hand caught on the edge of what was hidden beneath the mountain of packing Styrofoam, and he was so surprised he jerked backward and nearly knocked her over. He reached in, found the other edges, and lifted out a large flat metal sign that read, *Jiffy Latrine.*

"Oh, my God," he said, his voice hushed. "Genevieve. You stole the man's sign."

"No. I painted him a better one, and traded him for this one. But don't keep this one outside or the marker will start to fade."

"I will never let it out of my sight. I will get wallet-sized pictures of it to carry with me everywhere I go."

"Happy Hanukkah, Jeremy." Genevieve leaned down and put her

arms around him.

He balanced the sign across the edges of the box, turned, and pulled her into his lap the way he had on the first afternoon of Winter Camp. Then he slid his hands into her hair, looked into her eyes for a long, quiet moment, then kissed her.

"You are the awesomest wench ever."

"I know."

"Please, please stay," he said softly, his lips moving over hers as he spoke.

"I was planning on it."

"For more than a night. As long as you want. I…" He stopped, looking out the window to his right. "It's after sunset. New day. We can start again."

"But I don't want to start over. I liked everything that happened with you before. And this week. And now."

He lifted one hand between them, his fingertips resting gently, the slightest touch, on her lips.

"I want more." His breathing was uneven. "I…I miss you."

She stared at him.

"I miss you a lot. I don't care if we never steal another sign or build canoe Stonehenge at the fire circle or go freeze our butts off making color war happen. I miss you, here." He gestured with his hand at the slight amount of space between them. "Not just at camp. Here, with me. The best times I've had in my life have been with you."

His hand gently traced her cheek, pushing another strand of her hair behind her ear.

"I love you, Genevieve. For years now. All that time, every summer we were together, it was perfect. But since…a while now, I wanted you. Then, after your parents died, and I went to school, and…I thought you might not want to be around me, around the reminder of what happened."

He looked down suddenly, and Gen ducked her head until she met his eyes and lifted his chin so he looked at her again.

"I'm sorry I didn't tell you why I was leaving, that I was going to school. And that I didn't call you or try to see you when you got back from Iceland. I was stupid."

"No, that was me yesterday, when I wasn't sure if I should text you."

"You should totally text me. All the time."

"Yeah? Well, you should totally kiss me. All the time."

"I like your plan better."

They were still kissing by the door when the pizza delivery came. Gen agreed, after they demolished the entire pie, that it was probably the best pizza ever, second only to Nadine's. She helped him clean up all the scattered pieces of Styrofoam that had migrated across his carpet.

Jeremy showed her parts of his apartment, like the cubby he'd "borrowed" from one of the cabins, refinished and turned into a cabinet for his movie collection. He had different mementos of their adventures, too. A flat piece of metal with faded numbers on it turned out to be a scrap from one of the canoes they'd moved all around camp one summer. A rock she'd painted last year during rainy day arts and crafts showing a golf cart parked on top of the flagpole—a feat they'd never figured out how to pull off—sat on the table near the sofa.

Then she noticed his menorah in the corner cabinet.

"You made that back when we were ten or eleven, right?" She opened the door and pulled it out, the thick blue and green glaze cool under her fingers.

"Yeah, I think so. I didn't have one, so I borrowed it from my mom."

She held it closer to her. "Do you have candles?"

He nodded.

"Can we light it?"

He swallowed, then nodded again.

It took some whittling of the wax with a butter knife, but eventually they fit eight candles into the uneven holes. "I think I used a pencil eraser to make those holes. No candles are that small," Jeremy said, thin twists of wax falling from between his fingertips as he sharpened the bottom of a Hanukkah candle. "What was I thinking?"

"I like it." He shook his head and passed her the last candle. Gen lit a match, and together, his arm around her shoulders, her hands around his waist and her head tucked under his chin, they said the blessings.

She stopped after the second, but Jeremy continued, his low voice surrounding her and moving through her as he said the prayer that honored miracles and unexpected joy. "*Baruch ahah adonai, eloheinu melech ha'olam shecheyanu v'kiymanu b'higyanu lazman hazeh.* Blessed are you, Lord our God, King of the Universe, who has granted us life, sustained us, and brought us to this day."

Gen finished the prayer with him, her voice barely above a whisper. "Amen."

When he kissed the top of her head, she looked up at him. "It's not the first night."

"No, but it's pretty miraculous."

"What is?"

"You're here. There's nothing I've ever wanted more."

In his arms, and in his home, Gen felt safe. She didn't think before speaking because she didn't need to. "I love you."

He breathed in slowly, as if he wanted to bring the air that carried her words inside of himself. "Another miracle."

"If I stay the night, there's no way Scott can interrupt us."

Jeremy lifted his head, a huge grin spreading across his face. "EPIC!"

Gen laughed. "Wow, almost a whole hour without yelling about something being epic."

"Yet another miracle."

"Your neighbors must hate when you do that."

He shook his head. "Nah, there's not much that's epic without you." Then he leaned down and kissed her like breathing was entirely unnecessary.

The light of the menorah danced on the walls amid the sound of laughter, the crackle of chocolate wrappers, and the crunch of graham crackers. They talked about the northern lights, the stars out his window, and the flakes of snow that blew past. Then, as the candles burned low, the shadows of two people merged into one before the lights went out.

THANK YOU

Thank you so very much for reading *Lighting the Flames*. I hope you enjoyed it.

If you did, or if you didn't, I welcome your review at whatever location you prefer, with as many or as few animated gifs as you like. If you elect to review this book, I am grateful. Thank you.

If you'd like to read more fiction that I write, I invite you to subscribe to my Hey I Wrote Another Book mailing list:
http://eepurl.com/-5-Cf

I shall contact you with brevity and some hilarity in the event that I write another romance. If you'd like to tell me that I should write one RIGHT NOW, please do feel free to email me:
sarah@smartbitchestrashybooks.com.

This project began because I have a rule: I'm not allowed to complain about the same thing twice. If I do, I have to either shut up, or do something about it. This was my way of doing something about the lack of holiday fiction that featured Hanukkah. I hope that you enjoyed it.

May we all live happily ever after, in every season.

ABOUT THE AUTHOR

Sarah Wendell is the co-founder and current mastermind of the romance review and commentary site *Smart Bitches Trashy Books*. She's the author of *Everything I Know About Love, I Learned From Romance Novels*, and the co-author of *Beyond Heaving Bosoms: The Smart Bitches' Guide to Romance Novels*.

This is her first full-length piece of romance fiction.

To find Sarah online
Twitter: @smartbitches
Facebook: TrashyBooks
www.smartbitchestrashybooks.com
sarah@smartbitchestrashybooks.com

ALSO BY SARAH WENDELL

Beyond Heaving Bosoms: The Smart Bitches Guide to Romance Novels

Everything I Know About Love, I Learned from Romance Novels

And every day, there's something new at SmartBitchesTrashyBooks.com, where we talk about romance genre, and the intelligent, marvelous women who read and write it. Come join us!

Made in the
USA
Middletown, DE